Hurt him or he'll take your girl

It seemed as though they had spotted each other at exactly the same moment. There was Jake, across the room bussing tables, glancing at them furtively. Brad glowered at Jake, and suddenly the voices screamed in his brain.

Hurt him or he'll take your girl.

Why was Jake working at the club this night of all nights? Brad wondered. Was he spying on them? Was he planning revenge?

"Brad, what's the matter?" Cassie asked.

"Oh, I'm sorry," he said happily, brightening his expression for Cassie's sake. "I was drifting. Thinking about you and me."

Hurt him or he'll take your girl.

Don't miss these other books
by **Nicholas Adams**

The *Horror High* series

#1 Mr Popularity
#2 Resolved: You're Dead
#3 Heartbreaker
#4 New Kid on the Block
#5 Hard Rock
#6 Sudden Death
#7 Pep Rally
#8 Final Curtain

I.O.U.
Santa Claws
Horrorscope

Available from HarperPaperbacks

HORROR HIGH

Mr. Popularity

Nicholas Adams

HarperPaperbacks
A Division of HarperCollinsPublishers

HarperPaperbacks *A Division of* HarperCollins*Publishers*
10 East 53rd Street, New York, N.Y. 10022

Copyright © 1990 by Daniel Weiss Associates, Inc.
and Coleman Stokes
Cover art copyright © 1990 by Daniel Weiss Associates, Inc.

Produced by Daniel Weiss Associates, Inc.
33 West 17th Street, New York, New York 10011.

First printing: November 1990

Printed in the United States of America

HarperPaperbacks and colophon are trademarks of HarperCollins*Publishers*

10 9 8 7 6 5 4

Mr. Popularity

Prologue

Brad Forester felt alive in the dark of the night. His heart pounded with a savage beat. For a short while, at least, he could pretend that he was relieved of his burden.

The creature moved next to him. They were one, beasts at heart, by nature. They were both sleek and dangerous.

The estate was big enough for him to roam freely in the night. He felt safe, protected by the darkness. No one could see what he was doing.

Their legs carried them through the trees. Bits of wet dirt and leaves stuck to the bottom of his bare feet. Sweat poured from his naked chest, even in the coolness of early spring.

The panther beside him came to a sudden halt. He stopped beside it and tensed as its deep black eyes peered straight ahead into the shadows.

A low growl whirred in the back of the animal's throat. It saw something that escaped his human eyes. He envied the beast, so pure and black.

They moved forward slowly. The darkness seemed to wrap around his sweating body, hiding all of his sins and wrongdoings. There was escape in the darkness, sanctuary under a night sky.

In the cloak of shadows, he wrestled with demons and memories, some of which were only vague impressions in his tortured psyche. The beast touched its wet nose against his skin. It was the only thing that truly loved him.

His hand stroked the long, smooth neck. The animal purred. He had raised it himself from its birth. Now it was majestic and proud, a kindred spirit from the wild. Neither one of them could be tamed, not even when they visited the grave together.

He stumbled slowly toward the sacred ground. The visit always brought intense pain.

The panther stayed behind him. It lay on the ground, seeming to know that it was not part of the ritual.

He stopped beside the grave. She was lying beneath the dirt, waiting to speak to him. He could hear her voice as if she still lived and breathed.

Hello, Brad.

But he could not speak. Her sweetness almost killed him. He came again to offer his sorrows. But the girl beneath the ground would not accept them.

No, Brad, that's not what I want.

Her voice repeated over and over in his head. The pain became too great. He fell to his knees.

I'm sorry, Brad, it's just not working out.

Her image appeared in his head. He saw her light-brown hair. The blood was trickling from her mouth.

Then the shadow fell over them. It was dark

and sinister. He turned, but there was no one there.

He opened his eyes. The other voice had come into his head. It was low and evil. He always heard it before he was going to do something wrong.

She had it coming.

"No."

His head shook violently. He wanted the hateful voice to go away. But it continued to torment him.

She had it coming.

"Stop it."

No, Brad, that's not what I want.

He put his hands on his temples. He wanted to squeeze out the voice. If he could make it go away, he would be pure again.

The little tramp.

I'm sorry, Brad.

He put his face in his hands. Tears poured from his eyes and he fell forward into the dirt.

I can't see you anymore, Brad.

She had it coming.

"Stop it!"

He writhed on the ground in his agony. His body was smeared with dirt and leaves. He cried until his soul was raw, but he could not cry enough to make the voices go away.

I'm sorry, Brad.

The little tramp.

Something cold pressed against his bare back.

"Alice?"

It was the creature. It had come closer to him. His eyes turned upward toward the sky.

Streaks of dull light were already forming dusty shafts in the trees. The creature was telling him that daybreak was near. It was time to retreat into their hiding places.

He stood up. His body felt numb. But his head still whirled with the heavy crashing of the voices.

I'm sorry, Brad.

The little tramp.

The shadow appeared over his shoulder. He turned to see the figure, but it was gone again. And she was lying there in the pool of blood.

She had it coming.

I care about you, Brad, but I can't see you.

He started for the large house.

As they came closer to the stone walls of the house, the creature began to nose the air. He led it down to the basement and slipped the chain around its neck, keeping it hidden and safe for another day.

The animal always fed after their romp. From a bag, he poured dried food into a bowl.

"Tomorrow," he said to the animal. "I'll see you tomorrow."

As he came out of the basement, he saw that the sun had almost risen. He could still hear her voice. It echoed like a deadly siren's call inside his head.

Please, Brad. Please don't.

Her voice reminded him of how sour everything had become. He saw her lying there. The shadow came. He winced as the pain returned.

The other voice came back.

Bury her in the trees.

Please, Brad. Please don't.

Bury her, you fool!

The voices confused him. He wanted to do what was right, but sometimes they would not let him. He was prodded to do things that hurt people.

He lifted his hands toward her grave. "Please, Alice. Please. You understand, don't you? I love you, Alice."

No, Brad, that's not what I want.

The little tramp. She had it coming.

Her face loomed in his mind. He saw the glint of the friendship ring. Her eyes looked so sad.

I care about you, Brad, but I can't see you.

Her face was so perfect. But the blood was trickling from her mouth. She was dead at his feet, lying there.

Bury her in the trees.

You must never tell.

They'll hurt you if you tell.

"No!"

His voice echoed over the grounds. He looked up. His face was frozen with fear. What if someone had heard his cry?

His vision was blurred for a moment. His head ached with the pressure of a thousand hammers. He turned back, gazing toward the house. No one had risen yet. Even the cook was still asleep.

He slipped into the kitchen without anyone

hearing him. His parents were both heavy sleep-
ers.

*Take a shower, you idiot. Get the blood off your
hands!*

He bathed in the servant's shower adjacent to
the kitchen.

When he was clean, he slipped upstairs to his
own room.

"I love you, Alice," he said to the shrine he had
erected to her.

No, Brad, that's not what I want.

You killed her.

Bury her or they'll hurt you.

He lay on his bed, gripping the sheets like a
frightened child on a roller coaster ride.

He tried to close his eyes.

Brad Forester had to put the monster to sleep
for a few hours.

Only then would he be able to show his other
face, the face of Mr. Popularity.

Chapter 1

Cassie Arthur's brown eyes lifted to the clock on the pink wall of her room. "Oh no! I'm going to be late."

She had to leave home early if she was going to make it to Pelham Four Corners on time. The bus came at seven-fifteen. It was already twenty minutes before seven. Cassie had to hurry, otherwise she would miss seeing Brad. Usually she picked up the bus at Colony Road, about five minutes away. But she was willing to walk a little farther to be at the stop that Brad passed every morning.

"Cassie!"

Her door swung open. Cassie's younger sister peeked into the room. Andrea Arthur was a blond-haired, blue-eyed girl of twelve.

"You're up early," Andrea said. "I wonder why?" She wrinkled her nose and smirked.

Andrea knew why Cassie had gotten up early. She just wanted to tease her older sister.

Cassie picked up her hairbrush. "I thought I told you to knock before you came in here."

She started to brush her hair. Cassie had wavy, shoulder-length hair that was easy to manage. She wore blue jeans, black pumps, and a peach and gray cotton blouse. She wanted to look good for Brad. Yesterday he had all but promised her a ride to school—if she was ever at the Pelham Four Corners bus stop when he drove by.

Andrea watched her. "Mom told me to wake you, but I knew you'd be ready. You're going to Four Corners to wait for Brad."

"Grow up, Andrea."

"You'd really walk all that way just to meet Brad? I hope I don't get like that when I'm sixteen."

"You will," Cassie replied. "If you like somebody, you'll—oh, why am I telling you this? Get out of my room."

But Andrea did not go.

"You look great," Andrea said. "Brad will think you're the prettiest junior girl at Cresswell High."

Cassie bit her lip. "Do you really think so?"

Andrea nodded. "You look wonderful, Cassie."

Cassie studied her smooth cheeks. She did look pretty even though she wasn't wearing any makeup. Her beauty was natural. She was not as flashy as some of the other girls at Cresswell, certainly not the glitzy cheerleader types, who were all smiles and hairdo.

"Andrea! Cassie! Breakfast is on the table."

Her mother's voice echoed through the house. They had moved to a small, two-story, single-family house in the Upper Basin after Cassie's widowed mother had been promoted to director of services at the Cresswell Country Club. The job had brought with it a substantial raise, as well as longer hours away from home.

"Cassie!" her mother called again.

"Coming, Mom!"

Andrea turned toward the stairs. "She wants to leave early so she can chase Brad Forester!"

Cassie glared at her sister. "Out!"

"Brad 'n' Cassie, Cassie 'n' Brad."

"I mean it, Andrea!"

Andrea giggled as she hurried downstairs.

Cassie glanced at the clock again. She had to go. If Brad was early, she might miss him altogether. She picked up her books and went downstairs to join her mother and sister.

Mrs. Arthur was waiting in the kitchen. She always got up to make their breakfast, even though her job at the country club often kept her there well past midnight.

"You look nice today, Cassie."

Cassie reached for a piece of wheat toast. "Thanks, Mom. I'm off."

"Hold on," her mother said in a concerned tone. "I want to hear about you and Brad Forester."

Cassie scooped scrambled eggs onto the toast, folding it into a sandwich. "I'm really late, Mom."

"School doesn't start until eight," Mrs. Arthur replied. "You've got another half hour before your bus comes."

"Mom—"

Andrea smiled impishly. "She's not catching *her* bus. She's going to Four Corners to wait for Brad Forester."

Cassie shot an angry look at her sister. "Why don't you mind your own business, Andrea?"

Mrs. Arthur broke up the argument. "Be nice, both of you."

"I have to go now," Cassie practically pleaded, "or I'll be late."

Mrs. Arthur shook her head. "Cassie, do you really think it's wise for you to chase after Brad Forester?"

"I'm not chasing him," Cassie insisted.

"His father is my boss," Mrs. Arthur went on. "He's president of the country club. He's also the one who promoted me."

Cassie remembered the party that Mr. Forester had given for her mother's promotion. Brad had spoken to Cassie for the first time at the party. He had even chatted with her a few times in chemistry class. But Brad still remained distant and aloof with her. Even though he was the most popular boy in the junior class, it seemed to Cassie that he was waiting for her to make the next move.

Mrs. Arthur began to straighten the collar on Cassie's blouse. "I know things are different than they were in my day, but you still shouldn't go chasing after boys."

"It's not like that, Mom. Brad just said that if I was ever at the bus stop when he passed, he would give me a ride to school. Besides, I have to check with him about some chemistry homework before school starts."

Her mother sighed. "I just want the best for you, honey."

Cassie tried to smile, though she was aware of the clock on the kitchen counter. "I've got to go, Mom, or I'll be late."

"Well, just keep in mind that Brad's father signs my paycheck. He also owns most of the town. Everything you do reflects on me, remember that."

"Nothing's going to happen, Mom. Don't worry."

Cassie ate the toast-and-egg sandwich in three bites. She grabbed a glass of orange juice from the table and gulped it down. Her brown eyes stole another look at the clock on the kitchen counter. It was six-fifty. Cassie had to leave now if she was going to make it to Pelham Four Corners on time.

She started for the front door.

"Be careful," Mrs. Arthur called. "I don't want you to end up like Alice Gilbert!"

The door slammed behind Cassie. Her mother always invoked the name of Alice Gilbert when she wanted to put a cautious fright into her girls. Alice Gilbert, a sophomore at Cresswell High, had mysteriously disappeared a year earlier, shocking the town.

Cassie and Alice had been in the same class at Cresswell. So far, no one had been able to find the poor girl. After her disappearance, Alice's face had been printed on a milk carton, but still there was no trace of her.

Cassie moved along Garden Street through the Upper Basin. The neighborhood was not the nicest section of Cresswell, but it was better than the Lower Basin, the bordering community. At least the residents of the Upper Basin made an effort to trim the shrubbery in their front yards. The Lower Basin was mostly warehouses and three-story tenements.

As Cassie passed the Laundromat, she checked the time on the big clock over the dryers. Seven o'clock. She might not make it to the bus stop in time.

Cassie knew an alleyway she could cut through. The shortcut would take her all the way to Bryant Park, the unofficial border between the Upper Basin and a small shopping district that led into Pelham Four Corners. Once she got to the park, it was a short walk to the bus stop.

Once, Cassie would have figured she didn't have much of a chance with Brad. But he obviously liked her, considering that he'd talked to her more in the past three weeks than ever before. And she knew he didn't have a girlfriend. The girls he dated from time to time were not the type who wore loads of makeup and jewelry either. So, all things considered, Cassie knew that she had a better than average shot at going out with the most popular junior boy in school.

Everything would be fine, Cassie told herself, as long as she made it to the bus stop on time this morning. Brad couldn't pass the bus stop without seeing her. She would make sure of that. Then he would stop and offer her a ride. And then he would ask her to go out.

Cassie stopped on Garden Street. She had reached the alleyway that formed the shortcut to the park. She had never walked through the alley before. But her mother had made her late so she had to risk it if she was going to see Brad.

Cassie turned into the alley. Suddenly the shadows engulfed her. The air felt cool and damp and stale.

She took a deep breath. Except for Alice Gilbert disappearing, nothing so terrible had happened to any of the students at Cresswell High School. She would be safe in the alley. After all, it was broad daylight.

Cassie started to walk fast. The alley was about a hundred feet long, dark, and winding, so it was impossible to see from one end to the other, and barely wide enough for a small car to pass through. The park was on the other side.

Brad Forester was worth it. Cassie hurried in the shadows. She was halfway down the alley when a dark figure stepped out of the shadows to block her path.

Chapter 2

Cassie stopped. She wanted to back away, but her legs were stiff. The impulse to scream overcame her. Her lips parted, but the panic would not allow her voice to escape.

The figure moved toward her. It was a tall, lanky man, his features shrouded in darkness. She thought of Alice Gilbert again.

"Stay away from me!"

The strength came back into Cassie's legs. She turned to run. Her feet got tangled beneath her, and she felt herself falling.

"Cassie!"

Hands caught her before she hit the ground. Strong fingers gripped her arms. She struggled to get away.

"Cassie, it's me!"

She stopped struggling. The voice sounded familiar. Where had she heard it before?

"Cassie, it's me. Jake!"

His face caught the light. A shock of sandy hair fell over his forehead. He smiled at her. He was wearing a varsity track sweater from Cresswell.

"Jake?"

"Jake Taylor," he replied, smiling. "You know

me. We're in the same chemistry class. First period."

Cassie's mouth hung open. The tightness left her chest. She could breathe again, but she was still speechless for the moment.

"I work for your mother at the country club," Jake went on. "I'm a busboy. You know me. I run the mile for the track team."

Cassie gulped air, putting a hand to her throat. "Jake, thank goodness it's you. I was so scared."

Jake smiled. "You shouldn't be walking through here. There are a lot of dangerous scumpuppies hanging around in these alleys."

Cassie nodded. "I know. What are you doing here, anyway?"

Jake smiled. "I was just changing the oil in my new car. Have a look. I bought it myself. Earned every penny."

Jake gestured toward a green '79 Chevy that looked like a scarred battle tank.

"Shiny, isn't it?" he said proudly.

Cassie nodded, glad that Jake had been the one in the alley. Jake was also from the Upper Basin. He lived near Cassie with his mother and three younger brothers and sisters.

Jake was still smiling at Cassie. "How come you're walking through here?" he asked.

"I'm walking to Four Corners to meet some friends," Cassie replied. "Looks like I'm going to be late, though."

Jake pointed toward his car. "I'll give you a ride. I'm all finished."

Cassie thought that Jake had saved the day.

"Oh, would you, Jake? That would be so sweet. You're such a friend."

Jake winced at the word *friend*. He wanted to be more than friends with Cassie. He had been carrying a torch for her since they were in ninth grade together. But Jake had never been able to express his feelings for her.

Jake opened the door on the passenger side for Cassie to get in. "I'll show you what this baby can do on the street," he said through the open window. "It's faster than it looks."

He raced around the car and jumped into the driver's seat. The engine roared to life, pouring black smoke into the alley. Cassie coughed as she fanned the smoke away from her face.

"I do all my own engine work," Jake said over the noise of the motor.

Cassie nodded. "Aren't you the vice-president of the auto-shop club?"

"Treasurer," Jake said proudly. "But I'm not going to be a mechanic when I graduate. I'm going to college. I don't make straight A's but I have a solid average."

Cassie thought he was sort of cute and sweet. Jake was a good kid. She remembered that her mother had spoken highly of him.

Jake put the Chevy in gear. "Let's go."

The Chevy belched smoke as it rolled down the alley. She wondered if she was going to make it in time to see Brad.

"Do you like my car?" Jake asked.

Cassie thought it looked like a green monster,

but she nodded agreeably. "It's nice. When did you get it?"

"A few weeks ago. I've been saving my money," Jake replied. "Took me all of last summer and most of this year. I got it for eight hundred, but I've done a lot to make it better. I even put a new tranny in her and then overhauled the engine. She's faster than she looks."

"What's a tranny?"

"A transmission."

The Chevy bellowed as Jake steered it onto the main street. Jake was hoping that Cassie would be impressed by him. He had long imagined her sitting beside him in his own car. Now that it was happening, it felt just right.

For weeks, Jake had been trying to get up the nerve to ask Cassie on a date. The junior prom was not far away. Now that he had his car, all he had to do was ask her.

"Jake?"

"Yes?"

"Do you know what time it is?"

He pointed to the clock that flashed in front of the Cresswell Savings Bank. Cassie saw that it was almost ten minutes after seven. She was cutting it close.

"Can you go a little faster?" she asked sweetly.

"No problem," Jake replied.

He gunned the engine to impress her. Blue-white smoke flowed from the exhaust pipe, leaving a cloud behind them. In another two minutes, they reached the bus stop.

"Here we are," Jake said. "Are those your friends?"

Some other students waited for the bus.

"Not exactly," Cassie replied. "I better go."

As she got out of the green car, the other students began to whisper.

"Hey, isn't that Cassie Arthur?"

"Yeah, I wonder what she's doing here?"

"She's riding with Jake Taylor."

"That car is pathetic."

"Yeah, but I think Jake is kind of cute."

Cassie closed the door on the passenger side. "Thanks for the ride, Jake."

"Cassie?"

"Yes, Jake?"

He took a deep breath. "Well, I was wondering if you might—I mean, if you're not—"

Cassie knew that Jake was going to ask her out. She didn't want to be impolite and turn him down. Instead of letting him finish, she smiled and waved good-bye.

"Thanks again, Jake. See you in chemistry."

She moved away from the Chevy, toward the other students who waited for the bus.

"Cassie?"

But she only looked back to wave again. Jake pulled the Chevy into gear and chugged off toward Cresswell High.

Cassie stopped a few feet away from the other students. Some of them smiled at her, but they were mostly freshmen and sophomores. She took out a brush and began to fix her hair.

Cassie's heart was pounding in anticipation of

Brad's arrival. She still remembered how he had told her he'd give her a ride if he ever saw her waiting at Pelham Four Corners. They had been chatting in chemistry class, and she had fibbed and told him that sometimes she took the bus from there. But she got the hoped-for response. He touched her arm and said, "I'll give you a ride sometime."

A flash of red appeared suddenly as a vehicle approached the stoplight at the end of the block. Cassie stood up straight, trying to smile. But the vehicle was only a red Saab, not Brad's mint condition 1984 280ZX.

"Bus," someone called.

Cassie turned to see the yellow school bus approaching the stop. When the doors opened, all of the other students got in. Cassie just stood there, watching the road.

The bus driver honked the horn. Cassie hesitated, gazing up at the driver, who gave her a quizzical look. Cassie waved him on, sending the bus away without her.

Chapter 3

Brad sat up in his bed. His body was damp with perspiration. He peered toward the clock on his desk. If he didn't hurry, he was going to be late for school. Brad was never late. He was always on time. Perfect people had to be on time.

Brad climbed out of bed, feeling weak in the knees. His nighttime romps always left him tired the next day. But he had to run in the darkness. It was the only thing that made him feel pure.

He turned toward the mirror over his bureau. His face seemed gaunt, hollow. A dull white pallor had replaced his usual robust complexion. Brad knew he couldn't look bad. The most popular junior boy at Cresswell High never looked bad.

Brad straightened his body, pointing a finger at the mirror. "You better shape up. Look alive, Forester. Another day in the—"

Brad cringed. The pain shot through his head. One of the voices came behind the pain.

She had it coming.

Brad steadied himself against his desk. He took a deep breath. He knew he was going to do something bad today. The voices always came before the evil.

No, Brad, that's not what I want.

"I don't care what you want, Alice."

He felt a sudden surge of energy.

You're the one, Brad. Look at you. So handsome. You're the one.

Brad saw himself in the mirror again. "I'm the one."

His face was now flushed with color. He was admired by all of Cresswell. The most popular junior at the high school. He had scored the winning touchdown in this year's homecoming game. Next year he was going to be co-captain of the football team.

The rest are suckers.

"Suckers."

Alice tried to break through.

Don't listen, Brad. Please.

You're the one, Brad.

"I'm the one."

She had it coming.

You're the one.

The pain eased in his head. Brad was an actor about to assume his role in the play. The image was the only important thing. If they ever found out the real truth, they would hurt him.

Suckers, kid.

Brad dressed in a green polo shirt, tan chinos, and penny loafers, no socks. His thick, black hair fell into place with a single swipe of the comb. The reflection in the mirror was cool, but something stirred beyond the image. He heard Alice Gilbert's voice again.

Please, Brad. Please don't be hurt. You'll find another girl.

He winced, balling up his fist, pounding the top of his desk.

She had it coming.

Brad hurried away from the mirror. As he emerged into the hallway, he heard something thudding against the wall downstairs. He crept along the banister, hesitating when he saw his father pointing a finger in his mother's face.

"You!" his father cried. "You were flirting with that kid all night. The one with all those teeth."

A strange smile had stretched across Brad's mother's face. "Yeah? Like you weren't looking at Miss Coatcheck 1990!"

His father grunted. "Just get out of my sight."

As his mother walked away, Brad hurried down the stairs, making for the front door.

"Hey! Brad-man!"

Brad turned to face his father. He offered a big smile and fought back the voices. He would never let on to his father what was really happening.

Mr. Forester offered a fatherly smile to his son. "Brad-man, how's it going? You still slaying the ladies?"

Brad laughed a little. "Sure, Dad."

Please, Brad. You'll find another girl.

If you tell, they'll hurt you.

His father reached into a drawer in the hall table. "Your report card came, Brad."

Brad nodded, trying to play the dutiful son. "How'd I do, Dad?" he asked enthusiastically.

"Straight A's," his father replied proudly. "You've got another five hundred dollars coming to you."

Brad watched as his father peeled off ten fifty-dollar bills from a wad of money. That was their deal: Straight A's equaled five hundred dollars. The money didn't mean much to Brad. He already had a credit card, a tab at the Club, and a generous allowance. This was just a little something extra.

"Five more big ones, Brad."

His father slapped the money into his hand.

"What will you do with it, son?"

Brad smiled, holding up the wad of bills. "I'm putting it all in my savings account, Dad. I never waste my money."

"Good boy. Saving for that old rainy day."

"You bet, Dad."

Their conversation was right out of those sitcoms that ran on cable television, the old ones from the fifties and sixties. Brad had studied the shows. He had to work at being perfect.

Mr. Forester put his hand on the back of Brad's neck. His palm was cold and sweaty.

"You're a good kid, Brad-man."

"Thanks, Dad."

His father was a physically imposing man. But he had never lifted a hand to hurt Brad. Brad knew his father would hurt him if he found out about Alice Gilbert.

If you tell, they will hurt you.

23

She had it coming.

Please, Brad. Please don't be hurt. You'll find another girl.

Brad tried to turn away, but his father wouldn't let him.

"Hey, Brad-man. You know, your mother and I are planning a cruise after school lets out. You interested?"

Brad feigned a look of concern. "I don't know, Dad. I haven't taken driver's education yet. There's a class this summer. I need the credit to graduate, and it'll bring my insurance down on the ZX."

His father guffawed. "Don't worry about that. It's nothing."

"I still need the credit, Dad."

The hand lifted from Brad's neck.

"You're a great kid, Brad. You want to cruise with us, you can go. If not, you can stay here and go to summer school."

"Thanks, Dad."

"You'll be a heck of a lot better than your old man, Brad. You hear what I'm saying?"

"Sure, Dad."

Brad turned toward the front door.

"Let me know if you need any more money, son. All you have to do is ask."

The front door slammed behind him.

Brad took a deep breath. Fooling people required a lot of energy, especially when the voices were there. His father was always the toughest one to deceive. What would Edward Forester do if he found out his son had buried Alice Gilbert on the grounds of their estate, the largest estate in Cresswell?

Please, Brad.

You're the one.

Kill him!

Brad flinched. A new voice had appeared. He had never heard it before.

Kill your father.

Brad felt his legs become wobbly beneath him. He stumbled toward the red 280ZX. The arrival of the new voice had stunned him. It was shrill and fuzzy, like the sound of a smoke alarm.

Kill him now.

"No. He's my father."

Kill him.

Alice Gilbert's voice tried to creep in.

Don't listen to it, Brad.

Kill your father.

"No."

He climbed into the ZX.

Kill.

He slammed the car door and put the keys in the ignition.

Kill.

Don't listen, Brad.

"Both of you shut up!"

Brad started the ZX. He threw the car into gear and roared down the long, gently curving driveway. His hands clutched the wheel, knuckles turning white. Cool air rushed through the sunroof, taming the voices for a moment.

Brad reached over and opened the glove compartment. He tossed his father's money in with the other crisp green bills. He always left money in the glove compartment.

Once someone had rifled his car, stealing over two thousand dollars from the glove compartment. Brad hadn't reported the incident to the sheriff. Why bother? There was more where that came from.

The ZX burst onto Pine Cobble Road, just below the estate. If he drove fast enough, the voices might leave him alone for the day. Sometimes it was hard to get through school and still maintain his image as Mr. Popularity.

The new voice seemed to laugh at him. The shrill cry was strong and clear. Brad felt the pain in his head again.

Sweat formed on his upper lip. He felt nauseated. His vision blurred for a moment and then came back into focus.

Kill him now.

No, Brad, it's evil.

Her voice seemed to be getting weaker.

The ZX cut through the winding road that led from Rocky Bank Estates to Pelham Four Corners. The new voice blared in his head. His eyes grew wide. He sensed a sudden rush of power.

Kill him.

"No!"

You're the one, Brad.

He listened, but suddenly Alice Gilbert's voice was no longer there. The new voice had taken over for the moment. Brad felt the strength of the new voice inside him.

A leering grimace had spread over Brad's face.

His eyes were wide. His heart pumped savagely inside his chest.

It was time for another sacrifice. Only through sacrifice could he feel pure inside. The purity of the new voice would guide him.

Kill, Brad. Kill.

The ZX drew closer to Pelham Parkway. The bus stop was visible ahead. A girl waited there, but Brad didn't see her.

Brad saw the little dog running out into the street.

Kill it now.

"She has it coming."

Brad turned the steering wheel. The car swerved toward the dog. Then the girl at the bus stop screamed.

Chapter 4

When Cassie saw the red 280ZX coming toward the bus stop, she looked up at Brad and smiled. The smile disappeared as soon as she noticed the eerie expression on his face. His eyes were wide and maniacal, his straight white teeth were flashing. Cassie barely recognized him.

Across the street, an older woman called out to a small Yorkshire terrier. The animal had run into the street from her yard. It had stopped a few feet away from the curb.

Brad's 280ZX swerved to the left, straight for the terrier. A horrible yelping resounded through the neighborhood. The dog rolled over and over, tumbling across the asphalt from the impact.

Cassie screamed. She put her hands over her mouth. The dog was lying motionless in the street.

Brad screeched to a halt. The brake lights were shining bright red.

The older woman ran across her yard to the street. She looked down at the poor fallen creature. Blood trickled from the terrier's mouth. The dog had stopped breathing.

The woman began to shriek. "Buffy!"

Cassie started toward the woman. Her eyes focused on the body of the dog.

"Buffy!"

The woman knelt down. She touched the lifeless body of her beloved pet. The animal's head had been crushed.

Cassie knelt down next to her. "I'm sorry. I'm so sorry."

"I had her eight years. Oh, no. Buffy!"

A shadow fell over them. Brad was suddenly standing there beside the corpse of the dog. He seemed as if he was about to cry.

The woman stood up, pointing at Brad. "You! You hit my Buffy on purpose. I saw you swerve right for her."

Cassie also straightened up, looking at Brad. The eerie expression was gone from his face. He was so attractive. Tears pooled in his beautiful dark eyes. He was like a little boy pleading to be forgiven.

"I'm sorry, ma'am," he said sadly. "I saw her run into the street. I thought she was going to run in front of me, so I tried to swerve to miss her. I didn't mean to hit her."

"Liar!" the woman cried. "I saw you. You steered right into her. You killed her on purpose."

"No," Brad insisted in a penitent voice. "I'd never hurt your dog. Why would I run over it? I love animals."

"Liar! You're a bald-faced liar!"

Tears rolled down Brad's face. He knelt to

touch the dog. He seemed as though he was almost on the brink of a breakdown.

His voice was so sincere, Cassie thought. His hands trembled as he stroked the dog's lifeless form. The accident had really upset him. How could the old woman not believe him?

"Killer. You murdered my Buffy. I'm going to have you put in jail."

Brad stood up again. He was speechless. Cassie could not believe he had killed the dog on purpose.

The woman started to pick up the body of her pet. "I had my Buffy eight years. And you killed her."

Brad reached toward the woman. He wanted to help. But the woman pulled away from him.

Suddenly a sheriff's patrol car was there. "What seems to be the problem?" the deputy asked as he got out.

"He killed my dog," the grief-stricken woman exclaimed.

Brad turned to the officer. "No," he said in an almost pathetic voice. "It was an accident. I swear."

"He deliberately ran over my Buffy," the woman insisted.

The deputy frowned at Brad. "Yeah?"

Cassie felt awful for Brad.

"It was an accident," he told the deputy. "The dog ran into the street. I tried to avoid it, but it stopped right in front of me. I wouldn't run over her dog on purpose."

The deputy rubbed his chin, looking at the life-less shape of the terrier.

"Let's calm down now," he said. "Everybody relax. I want you all to tell me what happened, one at a time and calmly."

"I'm telling you," the old woman said. "He ran over my dog. He did it deliberately."

"No," Brad replied, "it was an accident. Ask her," he said, motioning to Cassie. "She saw the whole thing. She was standing at the bus stop. Go on, tell him."

Brad touched Cassie's arm gently. Their eyes met. He seemed helpless. It had all happened so fast. Cassie couldn't believe that Brad had meant to kill the dog.

"Well?" the deputy asked.

Suddenly they were all staring at Cassie, wait-ing for her to corroborate Brad's story.

The deputy's narrow gaze was focused on Cas-sie. "Well, miss?"

They were all waiting for her to speak. She thought of what she had seen. It had happened too quickly.

"Tell the truth," the deputy urged.

Cassie shook her head. "No."

"No what?" the deputy asked.

"No, he didn't hit the dog deliberately."

"He swerved right at my Buffy!" the woman cried.

"Yes," Cassie replied, "but your dog ran out into the street."

"That's right," Brad said. "I tried to miss the dog, but it ran out into the street."

"No, you meant to hit her! I saw it with my own eyes!" the woman said.

Brad shook his head. "You've got to believe me, officer. I'd never do anything like that."

The deputy studied Brad. "You're Ed Forester's boy, aren't you?"

"Yes, sir."

"Scored the winning touchdown against City High," the deputy went on. "My little brother is Bobby Cochran."

"He plays on the line," Brad said. "He's a good blocker. I never would have scored that TD without him."

"Arrest him!" the grieving woman cried.

"He didn't mean to hit your dog," Cassie insisted. "It was an accident. Just like Brad said. The dog ran into the street. He tried to avoid it, but the dog ran right into his path."

That was how she had really seen it.

The woman pointed at Cassie. "You're a liar, too. You'll pay for your lies. You'll regret it."

"Take it easy," the police officer rejoined. "There's no need to get carried away."

"I'm sorry," Cassie said to the officer. "But I saw what I saw. I'm convinced it was an accident."

The deputy sighed, looking at the sobbing woman. "Ma'am, it's their story against yours."

She didn't reply. Her eyes were on the cold body of her pet.

"We do have leash laws in Cresswell," the deputy said. "You should have kept your dog tied up. If you had, then it wouldn't have been hit."

"No," Brad said to the officer. "Don't blame her."

Cassie beamed admiringly at Brad. His voice was so sincere, his expression so caring. He really wanted to reach out to the woman. Cassie felt a sense of relief.

"I want to buy her a new dog," Brad went on. "Any dog she wants. And I want to pay to have Buffy buried in a nice pet cemetery with a headstone and everything."

The deputy shrugged. "What more could you ask for, ma'am?"

"I'm really sorry," Brad said again. "If I could bring your dog back, I'd do it in a second."

The woman wasn't listening anymore. She walked away with the dead dog in her arms.

Brad looked into Cassie's eyes. He smiled weakly. Cassie smiled back at him. He was so nice.

"Thanks for backing me up," he said.

"You didn't mean to hit that dog," Cassie replied. She knew that what she said was more of a question than a statement.

Inside his head, the new voice was telling Brad that he had pulled it off. They believed him. The voice also told him to bribe the deputy. His father always took care of the law officers of Cresswell.

The deputy smiled at Brad. "She'll calm down in a couple of days. Probably take you up on that offer to buy her another dog. Sometimes people say things they don't mean when they're upset."

"I don't blame her," Brad said. "Officer, don't you want to check my car registration?"

"I don't think that's necessary. You didn't mean to hit the dog, so there's no need to report this."

Brad winked at him. "Go on, it's in the glove compartment. My dad would want you to do it. Just so there's no misunderstanding."

The deputy seemed to catch on. "Oh. I see. Well, maybe I will check it. I wouldn't want your father upset at me."

He started for the 280ZX.

Brad turned back to regard Cassie.

You'll find another girl, Brad.

The other voices were silent as he peered into Cassie's eyes. She had a glow about her, an angelic quality. Had he really found her again?

The deputy came back toward them. "Everything's okay, Brad. Your registration is fine. It's good for another two hundred days before you have to get it renewed."

Brad nodded and smiled. He knew "two hundred days" meant that the deputy had taken two hundred dollars from the glove compartment. Everything was square with them. Brad's father always said a bribe was like donating directly to a law-enforcement fund.

The deputy got into his car. He waved to them and drove off.

Brad and Cassie were alone. Suddenly there was an awkward silence. Then the new voice came into Brad's head.

She's special, like Alice.

Alice's voice was not far away.

Don't hurt her, Brad. Don't listen. She's a good girl.

34

She had it coming.

No, don't hurt her now that you've found her.

"I won't."

Cassie looked puzzled. "What did you say?"

"I said, um, do you want a ride to school?" he replied.

"Sure."

He started to turn away.

"Brad?"

He gazed back into her soft eyes. "Yes?"

Cassie blushed at his glance. "Well, I was just wondering . . . it's nothing, really. Just that, well . . . when I saw you driving down the road, you had this look on your face. Is everything all right?"

Brad felt a fluttering in his chest. She had seen the other side of him, but she didn't seem afraid.

She's the special one, Brad. Don't hurt her.

Cassie had a trustful expression on her face. She did resemble Alice. They were both so pretty.

Brad grimaced. "Oh, Cassie, it was awful."

Cassie hesitated. "What was awful?"

Tell her a lie. Make it good. She's special.

Brad said, "I was probably going a little too fast because I was late for school. Then this bug flies in through the sunroof. Whap! I got it right between the eyes."

Cassie shook her head sympathetically. "That *is* awful."

"If that wasn't bad enough," Brad went on, "I get another one. Pow, right in the mouth. Have you ever swallowed a bug?"

"No," Cassie replied.

He looked embarrassed. "Sorry, Cassie, I didn't mean to be so gross. But there I was with this bug in my throat and then that lady's poor dog—well, you know the rest."

He hung his head sadly.

"It's okay," Cassie replied.

Brad looked up. "It would have been a big mess if you hadn't helped me out. That was great the way you stood up to her."

"You didn't mean to hit that dog," Cassie replied. "I know that you're sorry. I can see it in your eyes."

Brad smiled broadly. Cassie had believed him. Suddenly he felt funny inside. Something else was stirring. Something he had not felt for a long time.

"I'll take you up on that ride to school," Cassie said. "If we don't leave now, we might be late."

Her voice was kind. She had a gentle manner. She was a lot like Alice, before that unfortunate evening when she had disappeared.

"Come on," Brad replied. "We can make it before the first bell."

They hurried toward the red car. Cassie climbed in on the passenger's side. What would everyone say when they pulled up to school together?

"Fasten your seat belt," Brad said.

Cassie buckled the strap. "This is a nice car, Brad."

He turned the key in the ignition. "Hold on tight."

As the car roared off toward Cresswell High School, only Alice Gilbert's voice was swirling in his head.

Don't hurt her, Brad.

She's special.

"I won't."

Cassie glanced to her left. "I'm sorry, did you say something?"

"I won't be late for school," Brad replied. "I'm never late."

"Punctuality is a good trait," Cassie said. "At least, that's what my mother always tells me."

Cassie leaned back in the seat. The car raced through the streets of Cresswell. She was finally riding next to Brad Forester. How long would it be before their first date?

"Are you okay?" Brad asked.

"Yes, thanks. I'm fine."

She was elated, in fact. Everything had worked out for the best. She had forgotten about the little dog and the blood that glistened on the black surface of the street.

Chapter 5

Jake Taylor cruised the junior parking lot in his green Chevy. He was looking for an empty space. The junior lot was almost full.

Most of the students at Cresswell High turned sixteen—old enough to drive—before their junior year. Like Jake, many of them had used their summer job money to buy cars.

Jake had saved for a year to get enough money to buy the Chevy. His mother had a good job as tax clerk in the Cresswell Town Hall. But if he wanted to drive to school, he had to earn his own money. Since his father died, there was little money to spare.

Jake worked Thursday, Friday, and Saturday nights as a busboy at the country club. The job and his studies kept him from having much of a social life, but he was hoping that would change now that he had a car.

As he drove slowly down the line of cars, Jake thought about Cassie. She was so pretty and sweet. He knew she didn't have a boyfriend. Even so, he had to hurry if he was going to ask her to the junior prom.

Jake began to get a little nervous. It was almost

time for the first bell. If he didn't find a parking spot soon, he might be late for chemistry class. The teacher was always angry at anyone who was tardy.

He turned at the end of the lot, starting along another line of cars on the back side. He looked at the clock on the dashboard. Five minutes before eight. He would have to park on the street if he didn't find a spot.

Smoke billowed from the exhaust pipe of the Chevy. Some girls pointed and laughed as they walked toward class. Jake ignored them. He was proud of his car. Of course it needed more work, but he'd do it once he had more money.

Jake spied an opening ahead of him, at the other end of the lot. He pressed down on the accelerator. The Chevy lurched forward like a tank going into battle.

Jake was feeling on top of the world. It was the first time he had driven to school. He would feel even cooler when he came back to his car at the end of the day. No more riding the school bus with the freshmen and sophomores.

The Chevy drew closer to the parking space. Jake started to swing wide so he could pull in, but a sudden flash of red turned the corner. A 280ZX whipped into the space ahead of Jake.

"Hey!"

Jake burst out of the Chevy. His face was flushed. He was ready to fight for his right to the parking spot.

Brad Forester got out of the ZX. He was smiling. He didn't even notice Jake until the other boy spoke.

"Hey, Forester, that's my parking place. You pulled in right in front of me. I was about to—"

Jake stopped in midsentence. His mouth fell open. The passenger door had opened. Cassie Arthur climbed out of the ZX, sinking his spirits.

She was with Brad. That was why she had wanted to go to the other bus stop. She had been waiting for him.

Brad stared at Jake. He saw the look in the others boy's eyes. Jake liked Cassie. It was obvious that he had a crush on her.

The voices kicked in inside his head.

He wants your girl.

Hurt him.

Keep him away from her.

No, Brad, that's not what I want.

Hurt him or he'll steal your girl.

Brad leaned against his car, trying to stay calm. "What's your problem, Taylor?"

"I was about to pull into that space," Jake replied. "But you whipped in without even looking."

Brad shrugged. "Hey, what's the big deal? I didn't see you."

"That's my spot," Jake insisted.

Brad appealed to Cassie. "Did you see him?"

Cassie didn't enjoy the tension that was growing. "Brad, maybe he was here first."

Brad flinched, fighting to keep his smile. "Yeah?"

The voices were raging.

She sided with him.

Brad took a deep breath. "I didn't see him, Cassie."

"No," Cassie replied, "we really didn't see you, Jake."

It hurt Brad to hear her say another boy's name.

You have to hurt him or he'll steal your girl.

Jake was fuming. He hated to see Cassie with Brad. What chance did he have with her if she started dating the most popular boy in the junior class?

"That's my spot," he insisted again.

Brad tried to stay composed in spite of the voices. He didn't want to show anger in front of Cassie. Alice Gilbert had been afraid of his temper.

She's special, Brad, the way I was special.

Hurt him or he'll steal your girl.

A pain cut through Brad's head. He could still hear Alice telling him how they had to keep their summer romance a secret. Her mother didn't approve of her dating Brad. Her mother disliked Mr. Forester.

Hurt him!

What if he lost Cassie? Lost him to Jake! Jake had to run track because he couldn't make the football team. He was a wimp.

Jake tried not to look at Cassie. He was trembling. But he would not back down, not in front of the girl he wanted to take to the prom.

"I want my spot, Brad."

Brad felt the beads of sweat popping out on his forehead. He wanted to crush Jake. The voices wanted him to do it. Brad knew he could take Jake in a fight. But he didn't want to scare Cassie away.

Cassie was anxious. "Brad, why don't we—"

"What seems to be the trouble here?"

The deep voice had come from Henry Lipton, the assistant principal of Cresswell High. Mr. Lipton wore a dark suit and a crew cut. He had a reputation for being hard on troublemakers.

Jake slammed his car door. "Forester stole my parking spot."

Mr. Lipton squinted at Brad. "Is that true?"

Don't lose it.

She's special.

Don't scare her away.

Cassie waited for Brad's reaction. His lips tightened into a winning smile. A friendly expression stretched over his face.

"It's no big deal, Mr. Lipton," Brad said. "I just pulled into the vacant spot. I didn't even see Jake's car. He started to blow a gasket over this, but I can park on the street. If he says it's his spot, I can get behind that. Okay, Taylor?"

Jake suddenly felt like he was the one on the spot.

Mr. Lipton glared at him. "Well?"

"I guess it's okay," Jake replied.

Brad gave a slight laugh. "Sorry, Mr. Lipton. It was just a misunderstanding. Jake didn't mean to act like a freshman."

Jake started to get back into his car.

Mr. Lipton frowned. "Wait a minute. Taylor, you can't park in the junior lot anyway."

"Why not?" Jake asked.

"Your car isn't registered," Mr. Lipton replied. "You can't park in the junior lot until you have a blue sticker on your bumper. There, look at Brad's car. He registered it properly."

Brad was beaming. Cassie shook her head. Jake was turning out to be such a goof. He had embarrassed all of them.

The first bell rang.

Mr. Lipton pointed toward the street. "Take it outside, Taylor. And I better not see this wreck in the junior lot again until you get a sticker."

Mr. Lipton turned toward the school office. "You have five minutes to get to class."

"Sure thing," Brad replied.

Cassie shook her head. "Honestly, Jake is such a baby."

Red-faced, Jake climbed back into his car. The Chevy belched smoke as he rolled toward the street. He would have to park on a side street, a couple of blocks away from school.

As he drove out of the parking lot, he looked into his rearview mirror. He could see Brad and Cassie walking toward chemistry class. They were holding hands. Cassie was laughing. She looked so happy.

Jake let out a defeated sigh. He didn't like Brad Forester, had never liked him. He didn't trust anyone who seemed so perfect.

His gut feeling went beyond his jealousy. He had seen Brad many times at the country club.

There was something creepy about Brad that made Jake afraid of him.

And Jake's fear would be justified as soon as he sat down in the chemistry lab—about thirty seconds after the tardy bell had rung. Cassie looked away, embarrassed for him. She knew the teacher was going to give him a hard time. Jake cringed in anticipation of his tongue-lashing.

"Mr. Taylor!"

Jake smiled tenatively at the young woman with prematurely gray hair. "Good morning, Ms. Koger."

Koger the Ogre was her nickname outside class.

"Mr. Taylor, am I correct in assuming that you earned your letter in track?"

Jake nodded. "Yes ma'am, I finished third in the all-county mile in March."

"Then see if you can bring yourself to run just a little bit faster from now on so you can get to class on time."

Jake nodded and turned toward the lab desks. All of the spots seemed to be taken. It was just like the parking lot.

"We're waiting, Mr. Taylor."

Jake shrugged. "I can't find a lab station."

"There's an empty stool by Mr. Forester," the teacher replied.

Jake exhaled. He wished that the lab seats were assigned. They had assigned desks for regular class, but the lab was always random seating. Now he had to sit next to Brad after the fiasco in the parking lot.

"Is there something wrong, Mr. Taylor? Do you have a good reason for holding up this class?"

The whole class was staring at him. Jake felt like an idiot. He couldn't remember when he had begun a school day with such rotten luck.

"Mr. Taylor?"

"Okay. Sorry."

Jake started back toward the lab station. He saw Brad's smile, but he couldn't warm up to his rival for Cassie's affections.

As Brad watched Jake come toward him, the new voice echoed chillingly inside his head.

Hurt him.

Jake sat down on the lab stool. "Why aren't you sitting with Cassie?"

Brad shrugged. "I like to sit in the back of the class."

"Sure you do."

If you don't hurt him, he'll take your girl.

"Koger the Ogre," Brad said.

Jake eyed him. "What?"

"She didn't have to come down on you like that," Brad replied.

Jake was suspicious. "No, I guess not."

"Hey," Brad went on in a friendly tone, "sorry about all that stuff in the parking lot. I really would have given you the space."

"Forget it, Forester."

"Shake on it?"

Brad offered his hand.

Jake sighed. "Sure, why not?"

He took Brad's hand. The skin was cold and

damp. Jake drew back his hand a little too quickly, but Brad didn't seem to care.

Jake looked away, grimacing at a dead bullfrog in a quart jar of formaldehyde.

Brad fixed his eyes on the jar.

"Keep that thing away from me," Jake said.

Brad drew the jar to his side of the lab station. His mind was racing. He knew that formaldehyde would burn. A whole quart would produce an explosion of searing flames.

Burn him.

Brad tried the stopper in the top of the jar. He was able to pry it loose with no trouble. He left it intact so Jake couldn't smell the fumes from the formaldehyde.

Jake looked toward the blackboard, trying to ignore Brad. He would never warm up to anyone who wanted to date Cassie. He had never realized just how much he cared for Cassie until he saw her with Brad.

Brad's blank face reflected in the depths of the frog jar. The frog was sacred, holy. It had gone from life.

The chemistry teacher tapped her pencil on the lectern. "Today we're going to study the nature of heat conductivity in metals. Would everyone please take the kitchen match I've placed at your lab stations. Light the match and then turn on your Bunsen burners."

Burn him.

Brad watched Jake all through the lab experiments. The voices kept urging Brad to action. But he knew he had to be smooth. It had to look like an accident.

"Brad, are you all right?"

He glanced up at Ms. Koger. "Yes, Ms. Koger. I'm fine."

"Do you know the answer to the last question?"

Brad stole a look at the numbers on Jake's calculator. "Yes, ma'am, it's twelve point five."

"Good. Now, let's apply this formula in a practical experiment. Turn up your lab burners again."

Jake sighed as the flame rose in front of him. Cassie hadn't noticed that Brad had stolen the answer from him. Instead she was gazing at Brad, adoring him from across the room.

Brad smiled back at Cassie. But he quickly returned his eyes to the frog jar. The formaldehyde would spread flames in a hurry.

"Now," Ms. Koger said, "take the wire in front of you and bend it out of its current, circular shape."

Burn him.

Burn him or he'll take your girl.

You found her, don't lose her to this geek.

He has it coming.

Jake had bent the wire out of shape. He started to draw the lab burner toward him. The flame burned deep blue as it came between them.

Brad reached for the jar. He loosened the stopper. It would be so easy.

Burn him.

Jake stuck the twisted wire in the flame. He stared intently as it turned into a circle again.

Brad knocked the frog jar forward. The volatile liquid splashed onto the burner. Jake screamed.

"Oh no!" someone cried. "Jake's on fire!"

The flames rose on Jake's arm, creeping up the sleeve of his sweater like a poisonous snake. He couldn't believe that Brad had set him on fire. He screamed again, waving his fiery arm in the air.

Brad's back was turned to the rest of the class. No one could see the maniacal look that had appeared on his face. His eyes were wide, and a strange smirk stretched tightly across his thin mouth.

Cassie pointed toward the lab station. "Brad, look out! The desk is on fire!"

Brad backed away from the flames, keeping his face hidden. The two evil voices were cheering inside him. The enemy had been vanquished, punished with the flames.

Jake swung his arm, but the motion only fanned the flames. He ran toward the front of the class, screaming. Someone moved to knock Jake to the floor. A loud woosh filled the lab as a cloud of white dust flew into the air.

Jake no longer felt the heat scorching his arm. The fire had been put out. Jake lay on the floor, stunned and afraid. His body shook from the bottoms of his feet. Brad had actually set him on fire.

"Are you all right, Mr. Taylor?"

He looked up to see Ms. Koger putting out the flames that had spread across the lab desk. She held a red canister extinguisher, flashing bursts of dry powder which put an end to the blaze. When the fire was completely gone, Ms. Koger turned back to Jake.

"Jake? Are you all right?"

Jake climbed to his feet. A large hole had been burned in the sleeve of his track sweater. His sweater was ruined, but his arm wasn't badly hurt.

"Jake? What happened?" Ms. Koger asked.

Jake's mouth hung open. He could not believe that Ms. Koger had not seen what had happened. Brad had clearly doused the lab burner with the formaldehyde. He had set Jake on fire deliberately because of their run-in that morning.

"I'm waiting," Ms. Koger said. "What happened back here?"

Jake's trembling finger pointed at Brad. "Ask him. He's the one who torched me."

Ms. Koger turned toward Brad. "What happened, Mr. Forester?"

The horrid expression had vanished from Brad's innocent face. He seemed as shocked as Jake. The "accident" had left him shaky.

"I—I'm not sure," Brad said.

"He turned over that jar!" Jake said excitedly. "The formaldehyde hit the flame of my burner. The whole place almost went up in smoke!"

"It happened so fast," Brad said. "I didn't mean to do it."

Ms. Koger squinted at Jake's charred sweater sleeve. "Are you all right?"

Jake took off his sweater. "I think so."

The skin of his arm had turned red, but the

burn didn't look serious. His arm stung where the fire had singed his skin, but he was going to live.

"You were lucky," Ms. Koger said. "The sweater took most of the fire. Now, tell me again, what really happened back here?"

"I told you," Jake started, "Brad—"

"I want to hear it from Brad," the teacher said.

Brad looked pitiful. "It was an accident, Ms. Koger. I—"

"Bull!" Jake said.

"Let him finish, Mr. Taylor."

Brad shook his head. "Thanks, Ms. Koger. Well, Jake said he didn't want the frog jar on his side of the lab desk. He thought the dead frog was creepy, so I moved it to my side of the station. I accidently knocked it over when I was reaching for my own lab burner. It could have happened to anyone. I mean, the jar wouldn't have been on my side of the desk if Jake hadn't asked me to move it there."

"Did you ask him to move it?" Ms. Koger inquired.

Jake's face turned red. "Yes, but—"

"You better go get that arm looked at by the nurse," Ms. Koger replied. "Brad, you come with me."

Brad nodded, innocently. "Yes, ma'am. I'm real sorry, Jake."

Jake turned away, heading out of the classroom. Cassie watched him go. A moment of doubt flashed through her mind. The accident with the dog and the fire were both weird. But Brad had had plausible explanations, and he seemed so apologetic and caring. He turned back to smile at her before he left the room. Cassie smiled back. All her doubts were erased.

After his arm had been treated, Jake left the nurse's office and started back to the chemistry lab. Ms. Koger met him in the hallway. She studied his bandage for a moment and then told him that he was expected immediately in the assistant principal's office.

"Brad's already there," Ms. Koger said.

Jake frowned at her. "Ms. Koger, it *wasn't* an accident."

She seemed to have suddenly become indifferent about the whole incident. "It's out of my hands, Jake. Sorry. I hope your arm feels better soon."

She turned away, heading back toward the lab. First period was almost over. Jake would have to get his books after he talked to Mr. Lipton.

As he approached the office, Jake could hear laughter inside. Brad's voice rose loud and clear from the enclosure. Jake knew he was in for another disappointment, but he still had to state his case. He knocked on the door.

"Come in," Mr. Lipton called.

Jake entered the office with his bandaged arm in front of him. Brad was sitting in a chair opposite Mr. Lipton's desk. Brad smiled at Jake as if they were old friends.

Mr. Lipton motioned to a chair next to Brad. "Sit down, Jake."

Jake eased into the chair but didn't look at

Brad. He didn't want to give the rich kid a chance to turn things around with his charm. Why couldn't anyone else see through him?

"How's the arm?" Mr. Lipton asked.

Jake shrugged. "All right. It still hurts a little. But the nurse said it will heal in a couple of weeks."

Brad made a whistling noise. "Whew, I was worried there, Taylor."

"Yeah, right," Jake replied curtly.

Mr. Lipton's eyes narrowed. "Jake, you and Brad had a problem this morning in the parking lot. And now this. Brad tells me he apologized to you in class. Is that right? Did he apologize?"

Jake felt another burning deep in his gut. "Well, I—"

"Did he or didn't he?" Mr. Lipton insisted.

Jake nodded. "Yes, he apologized."

"It was all a misunderstanding," Brad said.

"He did it on purpose, Mr. Lipton. He splashed the formaldehyde into my lab burner as I was pulling it toward me. It wasn't an accident."

Mr. Lipton leaned back in his chair. "That's a pretty strong accusation, Jake. Why would Brad want to do something like that?"

The explanation in Jake's head was suddenly muddled and vague. It seemed stupid to accuse Brad of being jealous of Cassie. And the parking lot confrontation seemed so far off and innocent now. He couldn't find the words.

Mr. Lipton was definitely on Brad's side. "Brad did apologize, Jake. And he told me he would buy you a new letter sweater."

Jake felt himself losing the battle. "Mr. Lipton, he tipped that jar into my lab burner. He had to aim it to set me on fire."

"Brad, do you have an answer for that?"

Brad held out his hands. "I was reaching for my own lab burner, Mr. Lipton. My watch got caught on the jar. I didn't mean to knock it over. Besides, Jake was the one who wanted me to move the jar to my side of the lab station. The jar wouldn't even have been there if he hadn't thought that dead frog was so creepy."

The assistant principle glared at Jake. "Is that right?"

Jake sighed, defeated. "Yes, sir."

"I'm really sorry, Jake," Brad went on. "I'm sorry that your sweater was burned. I'll be happy to buy you a new one."

Jake cast a hostile look at Brad. "I don't want your money."

Mr. Lipton leaned forward, folding his hands together. "Jake, that's a horrible attitude. Brad's offering to pay for something that's not really his fault."

"Yeah?" Jake challenged. "If it's not his fault, then why is he offering to pay?"

"Maybe he wants to be a good guy," Mr. Lipton replied. "He wants to do the right thing because you got hurt and he feels bad."

Jake looked down at the floor. He was so angry that he could no longer defend himself. Brad had slanted everything to make it look as if he were innocent of any wrongdoing. Mr. Lipton seemed convinced that the fire had been an unfortunate accident.

"I'm sorry," Brad said again. "That's all I can say. If there's anything I can do, Jake, just name it. I feel awful about this."

Jake shook his head again. "Forget it, Forester. I don't want anything from you. Just stay away from me."

Mr. Lipton exhaled and looked at Brad. "If you don't mind, I'd like to have a word with Jake in private."

Brad nodded, smiling. "Sure, Mr. Lipton. I'm really sorry about this. But it was an accident. I swear."

Jake gave a sarcastic laugh. Brad appeared to be wounded by the laugh. He offered a penitent frown before he left the office. The voices in his head were telling him that victory was at hand.

When Brad was gone, Mr. Lipton's face grew stern. "Look here, Taylor, I've about had it with you."

Jake's eyes grew wide. "Me? What did I do?"

"You keep trying to make trouble for Brad," Mr. Lipton replied. "And I won't have it."

Jake couldn't believe what he was hearing. "But—"

"Brad's record is spotless here at Cresswell. He doesn't need someone like you causing problems for him."

Jake held up his wounded arm. "I'm the one who was hurt, Mr. Lipton. *My* arm was burned, not Brad's."

For a moment, an expression of concern

flashed across the assistant principal's face. He seemed to soften a little. But he would not back off of his defense of Brad Forester.

"I'm sorry you got burned, Jake, but it was an accident. To suggest that Brad did it on purpose is ludicrous. I can't think of a single reason why he would do something like that. Can you?"

Jake felt a tightness in his chest. He could not put his feelings into words. His tongue was tied in knots.

"I didn't think you could," Mr. Lipton replied. "Brad's a good student. You should do more to follow his lead."

"Oh, you mean like setting my lab partner on fire?" Jake replied.

"That's enough," Lipton said, pointing at Jake. "Now you shape up, Taylor. I'd hate to see you in real trouble."

"Yes, sir," Jake replied. He knew that nothing he could say would convince Mr. Taylor that Brad had deliberately burned him.

"Now get out of my office and don't let me see you in here again."

As Jake started down the hall, the bell rang to sound the end of first period. The halls filled with students changing classes. Suddenly Jake saw Cassie Arthur coming straight toward him.

Cassie seemed genuinely concerned when she saw the bandage on Jake's forearm. "Are you going to be all right, Jake?"

Jake nodded. "I guess so."

"I was so scared," Cassie reported. "When I saw those flames on your sweater, I nearly died."

"Thanks, Cassie."

"Brad's awfully sorry," Cassie went on. "He didn't mean to spill that formaldehyde. I know he wouldn't hurt you. He was so upset that he couldn't even walk me to my next class."

Jake's spirits sank even lower. Cassie was not going to listen to any disparaging remarks about Brad. She had a terrible crush on him.

"My sweater was ruined," Jake said. "Thank your new boyfriend for me. Not that he cares."

Cassie frowned at Jake. "That's not very nice."

"Nice?" He held up his arm. "Everybody is forgetting that I was the one who got torched. Everybody feels sorry for Brad."

"He's really sorry," Cassie replied. "But it was an accident. And he's willing to buy you a new sweater."

"I don't want his money," Jake replied. "Cassie, please, you've got to listen to me. That was no accident in the lab. Brad did it on purpose. You've got to believe me."

Cassie's face turned angry. "Honestly, Jake, you're such a baby sometimes. It's sick to say something like that about Brad. Do you know where he is right now? He's giving up his study hall to tutor a sophomore in math. Brad is a terrific person."

He held up his arm again. "Argue with this."

"You're wrong Jake. Just stay away from me until you come to your senses. I mean it."

But when the final bell rang, things would only get worse for Jake Taylor.

Chapter 6

Cassie Arthur sat on the edge of her bed, thumbing through the yearbook from her sophomore year. Brad Forester was on nearly every page, smiling back at her. He was so handsome with his perfect teeth and thick hair. And he was going to be Cassie's new boyfriend.

She had written their names together all day. Cassie had never felt this way about anyone before. *Does love really make people this happy?* she thought to herself.

She turned to the page in the yearbook where Brad was featured with the starting backfield of the varsity football team—the only sophomore among the four. He was also in pictures with the honor society, the student council, the school newspaper and the yearbook staff. Brad would dominate the new yearbook, due at the end of April.

The junior prom was also coming up on the second Saturday in May. Cassie had no doubt that Brad would ask her to the dance. He probably would have asked her after chemistry class if the accident hadn't shaken him.

Cassie frowned and closed the yearbook. The

thought of the flames on Jake's sleeve made her frightened again. She also remembered the dog as it lay bleeding in the street. The day had been oddly bittersweet for Cassie.

But she finally decided not to let any of the unfortunate events of the day cloud her relationship with Brad. He had needed her support and Cassie had given it.

"Hey, wake up!"

Cassie was startled. She looked up from the dreamworld of the yearbook. Andrea was standing in the doorway of her room.

"You could knock!" Cassie said testily.

Andrea shrugged. "Sorry. You look dazed. Is something wrong?"

Cassie thought of Brad's smile. She wondered if Brad would call her tonight, and she smiled at her sister.

Andrea grinned. "Brad! You did it!"

A slight smile parted Cassie's lips. "He gave me a ride to school!"

Andrea squealed gleefully. "Cool!"

"He would have given me a ride home," Cassie went on, "but he had to go to the country club this afternoon."

Andrea sighed and gazed dreamily into the air. "The country club. Hey, you can call Mom at work, and if Brad's there, she can put him on the phone so you can—"

"Andrea, get real. Brad will call me. I'm sure of it," Cassie said confidently. "He asked for my number."

"Oh, that's so romantic!" Andrea replied. "Did he try to kiss you?"

Cassie blushed and looked away. "Honestly, sometimes you're so immature, Andrea. Grow up."

The telephone rang downstairs. Andrea ran ahead of Cassie, who hoped it was Brad. But it was only their mother. Mrs. Arthur wanted to talk to Cassie.

"Yes, Mom?"

"There's fresh chicken in the fridge, honey, along with potatoes and salad fixings. Make dinner for you and your sister and tell Andrea she's to do the dishes."

"Sure," Cassie replied. "Mom? Has Brad been around there today?"

Her mother hesitated. "Well, he was in and out about two-thirty. Did he leave school early?"

"I'm not sure."

"Cassie, he asked me about you."

Cassie's heart dropped a momentary beat.

"He asked if you had a date for the prom," Mrs. Arthur said.

Cassie covered the mouthpiece. A joyous expression spread over her face. She screamed silently at Andrea.

"Cassie?"

"Right here, Mom."

"Maybe you should go down to Cyndi's Dress Shop," Mrs. Arthur said. "Pick out a formal and put it on layaway. I'll bail it out at the end of the month when I get paid."

"You really mean it?"

Mrs. Arthur laughed. "Go ahead. I wouldn't mind if you got something that was on sale, though."

"Thanks, Mom. Bye."

"Cassie?"

"Yes, Mom?"

"Brad is a nice boy, isn't he? He's so polite, . . . but sometimes I'm not sure."

"He's fine, Mom. Don't worry," Cassie told her.

Cassie hung up the phone. She was so excited that she could hardly stand still. She began to dance around the living room.

"What?" Andrea said anxiously. "Tell me!"

"He's going to ask me," Cassie replied. "Brad is going to ask me to the prom. Mom said I can go down to Cyndi's and pick out my formal!"

Andrea squealed again and grabbed her sister's hands, twirling her in a circle.

Cassie broke away, heading for the stairs. "I've got to go down to Cyndi's right now. I hope I can find something on sale."

Andrea was right behind her. "I'll get my shoes on and go with you."

"Hurry up!"

Cassie ran into her room. As she reached for her sweater, she knocked the yearbook off the bed. When she picked it up, the page had fallen open to the sophomore auto-shop club. Jake stared out at her from the photograph. He was the treasurer of the club.

"Jake," she said softly.

Cassie suddenly felt worried about Jake Taylor. He had been burned, and his sweater had been ruined. Maybe she had been too rough on him in the hall after chemistry lab. After all, he had been upset when he accused Brad of deliberately trying to hurt him.

She went downstairs and opened the phone book to find Jake's number, then dialed. "Hello, Mrs. Taylor. This is Cassie Arthur, one of Jake's friends. Is Jake home? . . . No? Oh, I just wanted to talk to him about—about chemistry lab. . . . No, it's okay, you don't have to tell him I called. I'll see him tomorrow in school. Thanks, Mrs. Taylor."

She hung up the phone. Cassie knew that Jake's mother would tell him about the call. She wondered if Jake might get the wrong idea. He did seem to have a little crush on her.

"Cassie? I'm ready."

Andrea was standing behind her.

"Cassie? Is everything okay? Who were you talking to?"

"No one. Let's go."

There was no need to tell Andrea about the accident in chemistry lab. It would only spoil the mood of their shopping trip. Cassie wanted to enjoy her happiness.

She just hoped that Jake was all right.

Chapter 7

Cassie's first date with Brad was on Saturday night. Brad asked her to the movies. Cassie wanted to see a romantic love story. Brad wanted to see an action movie, but readily consented to go along with Cassie's choice. Afterward, they went to a small restaurant for hamburgers.

Brad was caring, sensitive, polite, attentive, charming, entertaining, and handsome. He was everything Cassie had hoped he would be. Cassie imagined that all eyes were turned toward them while they were in the restaurant. They looked fabulous together.

At the end of the evening, Brad took Cassie home, walking her to her front door. Cassie wanted him to kiss her good night, but Brad was almost too polite. He only smiled, acting shy as he clasped her hand tenderly before walking back to his car.

Cassie watched him as he turned to smile at her one last time before he got back into his red 280ZX. She thought he was the only true gentleman she had ever met. She loved him even more for not trying to kiss her or get fresh on the first date.

* * *

The voices were alive inside Brad. The evil voices were telling him that Cassie was special, the kind of girl who could really understand him. Alice Gilbert's sweet voice could not make him leave Cassie alone. She'd tried to convince Brad that Cassie was not for him, but Brad knew they were meant to be together.

Brad began to call Cassie every night to chat. At school, he walked with her between classes, sat with her at lunch, gave her a ride home when he wasn't in a hurry to meet his parents at the country club. They seemed like the perfect couple, although Cassie kept wondering why Brad never tried to kiss her. She was almost beginning to grow impatient with his restraint.

Jake Taylor watched their budding romance from afar. He thought that the best strategy would be to wait and watch. He knew that, in time, his opportunity for revenge would come.

Brad continued to be perfect in his innocent act. He always tried to smile and say hello to Jake, always convincing Cassie that he wanted to be friends with Jake, that all was forgiven.

Brad's methods were working perfectly on the rest of Cresswell High as well. Everyone but Jake had forgotten about the "accident" in the chemistry lab. There hadn't been any more unfortunate incidents to cast suspicion on Brad. The world seemed right again for everyone except the boy whose arm had been burned in chemistry class.

Mr. Popularity seemed untouchable. No one could find fault with Cresswell's favorite junior.

But the sight of Jake at a country club dance one night set the voices raging again.

It was a beautiful evening, and it was Brad's first opportunity to show off Cassie to his parents. At the end of one dance, Brad held on to Cassie for a moment, peering into her brown eyes. The voices had been silent all night. Brad's salvation was the slender, smooth-faced girl in front of him.

Arm in arm, Brad and Cassie flowed across the room toward his parents' table. Everyone watched them, happy to see Brad with a nice girl. The two kids just looked so good together.

Cassie decided Brad's good looks came from his mother. Mrs. Forester was a tall, handsome woman, whose once-refined features were now becoming haggard. She had been drinking all night.

Brad's father was a big man with a wide, red face and an overpowering manner. He smiled at Cassie every time he looked in her direction, which was often. She looked away, obviously embarrassed by his attention.

"Brad-man," his father said. "You two looked like a million bucks out there. Maybe I can get you on that talent show on television."

Brad grinned and winked. "Thanks, Dad."

He pulled out a chair for Cassie, who sat down next to Mr. Forester. Brad sat between Cassie and his mother. They were all quiet for a moment.

Finally Mrs. Forester offered Cassie a tipsy

smile. "Honey, where did you learn to dance like that?"

Cassie looked at Brad. "I just followed him."

"You both looked wonderful," Mrs. Forester replied. "He's a perfect kid, isn't he? Doesn't deserve me as a mother, that's for sure."

Mr. Forester glared at his wife. "Why don't you lay off the juice."

She only looked over her shoulder. "Where's that waiter? I need another drink." She got up to look for the waiter.

Mr. Forester rolled his eyes and then smiled at Cassie. "I'd better go with her. You kids need anything, just ask." He winked at Cassie before he left the table.

Brad nodded at his father, distracted by someone across the room.

It seemed as though they had spotted each other at exactly the same moment. There was Jake, across the room bussing tables, glancing at them furtively. Brad glowered at Jake, and suddenly the voices screamed in his brain.

Hurt him or he'll take your girl.

Why was Jake working at the club this night of all nights, Brad wondered. Was he spying on them? Was he planning revenge?

"Brad, what's the matter?" Cassie asked.

"Oh, I'm sorry," he said happily, brightening his expression for Cassie's sake. "I was drifting. Thinking about you and me."

Hurt him or he'll take your girl.

Chapter 8

The following Saturday at dusk, on the road to Indian Point, Brad spotted the green Chevy and pulled up alongside. He honked his horn and swerved from side to side, screaming wildly. There was an eerie, glazed expression on his face.

Holding steady to the wheel, Jake rolled down his window and shouted at Brad, "Are you crazy, Forester? Stop it!"

The voices were raging inside Brad. They told him to get Jake now, to run him off the cliffs that dropped into Lighthouse Bay. If he didn't stop Jake, Jake would steal Cassie from him.

Jake looked at the cliffs that appeared suddenly on his right. They weren't far from Indian Point. The road began to curve a little. Just then a large delivery truck rounded the bend, heading straight toward Brad's car.

"Forester!" Jake cried.

Brad geared down, slipping behind the Chevy. The delivery truck shot past them. Brad swung his car into the passing lane again, roaring up next to the Chevy.

"Race me!" Brad cried.

Jake shook his fist at Brad. "Are you crazy?"

"Race me!"

"Forget it, you psycho!"

"Chicken!"

Jake eased off the accelerator, trying to slow down. The road had begun to wind in a series of long curves that followed the angles of the cliff. Brad went after Jake again, cutting in front of the Chevy. Jake had to slam on the brakes. Just as he did so, the Chevy began to spin out of control.

Jake held tightly to the wheel as his car careened toward the cliff. It was fifty-foot drop to the waters of Lighthouse Bay. If he went over the edge, he would be killed instantly when he hit. His wheels began to spit pebbles as they slid closer to the edge.

Jake froze, waiting for the fall. The Chevy teetered like a seesaw on the lip of the rocks. He started to open the door, but when he shifted his weight, the car tilted backward. He had to lean forward again to keep from plummeting into the bay.

His wide eyes gazed out of the windshield. Brad was backing up in his direction. When he got out of the 280ZX, he glared straight at Jake with a horrible look on his face.

"Help me!" Jake cried.

A weird smile spread over Brad's lips. He got back into his car. The red vehicle began to back slowly toward the dangling Chevy, inch by inch.

Jake knew what Brad was going to do. "No!"

He tried to open the door again, but the Chevy tilted toward the water below. Jake threw his weight forward. The red car was still coming.

Brad intended to ram the Chevy and knock Jake over the cliff.

Good job, Brad.

"No!" Jake cried. "Don't do it, Forester."

Brad moved slowly, making his enemy sweat. He wanted Jake to suffer before he died. The longer it took, the more Brad could savor the victory.

Jake cried out again, pleading for his life. He clung helplessly to the steering wheel. But Brad only kept coming, inch by inch. He had to be careful he didn't go over the cliff himself.

Then Brad stopped. He saw the sheriff's patrol car heading straight for them. A moment later, it pulled up on the shoulder of the road.

The deputy gawked at the Chevy. "Hold on, boy. Don't move." He got out of the patrol car and slowly ambled on to the Chevy.

Quickly, Brad got out of his car. Luckily, the patrolman was the same one he had bribed before. Brad straightened himself, ready to go into his Mr. Popularity act. He knew he had to be convincing to pull it off.

Brad stepped up to the policeman. "I was driving by, officer," he said in a concerned tone. "I saw this guy in trouble."

The deputy shook his head. "He's in trouble all right. Hold on. I'll see if I can get you off that cliff," he called to Jake. "Don't move."

Jake didn't have to be told twice. He clung to the steering wheel with his body weight thrust forward. He felt sick inside.

"I wonder what happened?" Brad said convincingly.

"He was probably speeding," the deputy replied. "He took that curve a little too fast. See the skid marks?"

Brad nodded innocently. "I'd like to help."

"I've got chains in my trunk," the deputy said. "Maybe I can pull him back with the patrol car."

Jake watched anxiously as the deputy moved around behind the patrol car. Brad followed him, keeping up the helpful routine. Jake didn't care about Brad now. He just wanted to stay alive.

"Hurry!" he cried.

The deputy came around with the heavy chain in his hands.

"I can hook them to the bumper," Brad said.

"No!" Jake cried. "Don't let him do it."

The deputy walked away from Brad, stopping in front of the Chevy. He was careful as he began to fasten the chain to the bumper. Jake held his breath inside the teetering vehicle.

Brad bit his lip. He wished there was some way to sabotage Jake. But he couldn't make a move with the deputy there. The voices would have to wait.

When the chain was secured, the deputy moved the patrol car in front of the Chevy. Again Brad tried to reach for the chain, as if to adjust it properly, but the deputy told him to back away. He then attached the chain to the patrol car's rear bumper.

"Don't move," he shouted to Jake.

Jake was tense as the chain tightened. He

heard screeching metal as the rocks scraped the bottom of his car. The Chevy was dragged forward until the wheels popped onto the shoulder of the road.

Jake started the Chevy and put it in gear, gently rolling away from the drop-off. His hands were shaking. A wave of fear and anger surged over him like the whitecapped currents of the bay.

The deputy was already out of the patrol car. "You almost bought it, kid. Better let me have a look at your driver's license and registration."

Jake handed over the documents.

"You were hot-rodding, weren't you, Jake?" said the officer. "Trying out your new car, seeing how fast it would go?"

Jake gaped at the officer. "No, I—"

"I ought to give you a ticket for reckless driving," the officer said. "You could have killed yourself, Taylor."

"No, you've got it all wrong—"

"Excuse me," Brad interrupted. "That curve is a bad one, Officer. I've almost lost it there a couple of times myself."

The officer gave Brad a serious look. "You shouldn't be speeding either, Brad. Your father wouldn't like it if I gave you a ticket."

"I know," Brad replied, looking penitently at the ground. "I try to take it easy. Maybe you should check my registration again."

"Sure," the deputy said, handing Jake his documents. "We wouldn't want any problems."

Brad grinned, happy that the policeman had

accepted another bribe. For a moment, Jake and Brad were alone together.

"You don't have to do your innocent act with me," Jake snapped. "I'm on to you now. Someday that act of yours will fail you, and *you'll* go off that cliff."

He will tell Cassie.

Hurt him!

"Okay," the deputy said, coming back toward them, tapping his shirt pocket, "you can go, Taylor. But the next time we have a run in, I'm going to give you a ticket."

"Cassie sure would be upset if she knew about all this," Brad said as he started toward his car. "I think I'll go out to Indian Point. See you later, Jake. And take it easy."

Brad got into his car, heading off for Indian Point. Suddenly Jake realized what Brad had in mind. There was a pay phone at Indian Point, on the deck that looked out toward the lighthouse. Brad was going to call Cassie so he could tell his lies before Jake got to her.

Jake looked toward Indian Point. He didn't want to go out there with Brad on the prowl. He would have to think of something.

When he got home, Jake knew he had to call Cassie. After he had looked up her number, he dialed her house, only to get a busy signal. She was probably talking to Brad.

Jake's heart was jumping. What if she didn't believe him this time? Why should she? To her, Brad was Mr. Popularity. When would she see the

71

other side of him? And when she did, would it be too late?

Suddenly the busy signal was gone. Jake wasn't sure what he would say to her. He held his breath until Cassie picked up the receiver.

"Hello, Arthur residence."

"Cassie, it's me—Jake. You've got to listen to me."

Cassie hesitated at the other end of the line. "Brad said you might call. I heard about your accident out at Indian Point. Are you all right?"

"Yes, but listen to me. Brad tried to run me off the road. I swear it. I was driving my car when he—"

"Please don't, Jake," Cassie replied in a sympathetic voice. "You've got to stop this."

"I can't, Cassie. Brad is no good. He has one face that he shows to everyone, but I've seen another side to him. He's evil, Cassie. You've got to stay away from him."

Cassie sighed. "Jake, maybe you should see someone. Ask the nurse at school. She can see that you find some help."

"Help?"

"Jake, it's not right to accuse people of things they haven't done. I know you like me—"

"Cassie!"

"—and I like you, too, Jake, but only as a friend. Please, don't do this any more. It's embarrassing to everyone. I have to go now, Jake. Sorry."

She hung up the phone.

"Cassie!"

Brad had done it again. Like an evil witch doctor, he had charmed Cassie into believing everything he said.

Jake was tired of being pushed around. He wondered if he had the courage to stop Brad once and for all.

He needed to sit in the dark living room a while and think. The rest of his family had already gone to sleep.

Jake climbed the stairs to the attic door. He walked slowly and carefully. He didn't want to wake his mother. There was something in the attic that he needed. His mother had thought it was safely hidden, but Jake had found it one rainy Sunday while he was straightening up.

He fumbled with the key until the door squeaked open. The noises sounded terribly loud in the darkness, but no one stirred in the Taylor household. Jake stepped into the attic, flicking the light switch. A single bare bulb burned over the piles of boxes and the lone steamer trunk.

Jake unfastened the latch, lifting the top of the trunk. He fished deep in the contents of the trunk. When he felt the soft nap of the cloth bag, he lifted the heavy, iron-laden package. Printed in gold letters across the bag were the words: E. TAYLOR, MARKSMAN. Jake's father, Earl, had been an expert shot. Jake reached into the bag, taking out the thirty-eight-caliber Smith and Wesson.

The gun was clean and well oiled, not a speck of rust. Jake lifted the pistol, staring down the straight barrel. He had already made a serious decision. If no one else would stop Brad Forester, then he would.

He closed the trunk, restacking everything so his mother wouldn't notice. Jake tucked the pistol in his belt and zipped up his jacket so the gun couldn't be seen. Easing out of the attic, he started back down the stairs.

"Jake?"

He almost jumped out of his skin. "Mom. You scared me."

His mother stood at the bottom of the stairs. "Why were you in the attic?"

"I thought I heard mice up there," Jake lied.

"Oh, I hope they aren't back again. Will you set some traps tomorrow?"

"Sure. Good night, Mom."

"Good night."

He watched her go back into her room, which was on the first floor. When he was sure that she had fallen asleep again, Jake slipped down the stairs and went out the front door. He got in his car again and drove toward the Forester estate with the pistol still tucked in his belt.

At Pelham Four Corners, Jake had a stroke of luck. He spotted the 280ZX. Unfortunately, Cassie was in the passenger seat. Jake couldn't believe it. She certainly hadn't lost any time in going out with Brad after he had tried to commit murder.

Jake had to change his plans quickly. He didn't want Cassie to see him, but he still wanted to find some way to get back at Brad. Finding Brad out on the road might work to his advantage.

After following the red car for a few minutes, Jake realized that Brad was going out to Indian Point. They drove up the same road where Jake had almost met his fate. He wondered what sort of sordid lies Brad was telling Cassie about the incident. He knew that Brad was taking Cassie to the parking lot, which was large and poorly lit, with many dark corners for parking and being undisturbed.

Jake parked the Chevy about thirty yards back on the road, hidden from view behind some shrubbery. He got out of the car quietly and walked in the direction of the parking lot. The Smith and Wesson was tucked into his back pocket. He was sure he wouldn't use it, not with Cassie around, but he wanted to have it with him just in case.

At the parking lot, he snuck along the perimeter in the direction of the water. When he had almost reached the guard rail separating the parking lot from the beach, he spotted Brad's car. Keeping low and close to the protective shrubbery surrounding the parking lot, Jake crept up to the guard rail and approached the car from the rear. He stooped over near the rear bumper in order that Brad wouldn't be able to see him in the rear-view mirror.

He stopped, held his breath, and listened.

"You don't know what it means to me to have you with me tonight," Brad said.

Cassie turned her face toward Brad's and said something so softly that Jake couldn't hear it.

"Cassie?" Brad said with the mock sincerity that Jake had come to know so well.

"Yes?"

"The prom is only a few weeks away," Brad said. "I was wondering if—"

She looked up at him and their lips met.

Suddenly, Brad broke away.

"You don't know, Cassie. You don't know how it is to suffer," he said, pain in his voice.

"Suffer?"

"I've waited so long," he said in a strange voice. "I've waited for you. For someone like you."

"Brad, are you all right?"

"I need someone who understands me," Brad went on. "Someone warm and tender, someone who'll never leave me. Someone like Ali—like—"

Cassie put her hand on his shoulder. Suddenly Brad turned, wrapping his arms around her in a tight embrace. Tears were rolling down his face. He cried for a long time with his head on her shoulder. Cassie stroked his head as if he were a little child.

"Brad?"

"I'm sorry," he replied, taking his head off her shoulder to wipe his eyes. "I didn't mean to—"

Jake was almost sick to his stomach. He had experienced Brad's evil side and here Brad was putting on a crying jag . . . for what purpose? So Cassie would pity him? And fall into some sort of trap?

Had Brad almost mentioned Alice Gilbert's name a moment ago?

"Maybe we should go, Brad," said Cassie.

"Yes," said Brad. "I'll take you home."

A late moon was rising over Lighthouse Bay. Jake crept back into the shadows as Brad started the car. He was going to get to the bottom of this, once and for all. And in order to do that, he had to go to the Forester estate.

Chapter 9

Jake had parked near the Forester estate on a side street. After giving Brad sufficient time to drop off Cassie and come home, Jake got out of the car, taking the pistol with him. He stole toward a large stone wall that surrounded the estate. The barrier had to be ten feet high. There was a tree growing next to the wall, so Jake tucked the pistol in his belt and started to climb.

When he came even with the top of the wall, Jake rested in the vee of two large branches. He peered toward the mansion, which was dark until a light flashed on in an upstairs room. A tall figure walked in front of the window.

"Brad," Jake whispered.

Jake grabbed the pistol from his belt. Sweat dripped off his forehead. His hand was trembling because the pistol was so heavy. Suddenly he felt stupid. What was he doing at the Forester estate sitting in a tree with a gun in his hand? Did he really think that shooting Brad Forester was the answer to his problem?

He would never get away with hurting Brad. He would be put away for life because of a dumb, impetuous move.

Jake quickly unloaded the pistol, putting the bullets in his shirt pocket. He had to get down before someone saw him. He could be arrested for just carrying a gun. Jake hesitated when he saw another light come on in a downstairs room. He stared toward the mansion to see if Brad was the lone shape moving through the house.

A dark figure came out of the back door, moving around to the side of the house. Jake's heart began to pound. It had to be Brad. The figure disappeared into a side door that appeared to lead into the basement. A few moments later, Brad came out again, only this time he wasn't alone.

A long, graceful, black creature moved through the dim glow of the downstairs light, which spilled through the window. Both of them seemed to be heading toward a grove of trees behind the house. Jake started to climb down. He wanted to get a better look at the creature. Maybe this was just what he needed to blow the whistle on Brad. What did Brad have locked up in the basement, anyway?

When his feet hit the ground, Jake followed the curve of the wall. He reached the rear of the estate, stopping to listen for Brad. He stepped slowly until he heard a low wailing sound. Jake had never heard anything like it before.

There were no trees along the back boundary of the wall, so Jake had to find handholds in the stone in order to climb back up. He pulled himself up slowly, chinning to the top of the barrier.

Jake's eyes grew wide. Brad had thrown himself on the ground. He was wallowing in the dirt, making strange noises. He was moaning and beating the dirt with his fists. What was his problem?

Jake felt his fingers giving way on the wall. He tumbled backward toward the ground. A small cry escaped from his throat as he fell. He hit on his feet with a dull thud.

Suddenly a shrill, animal cry arose in the night. Jake scurried to his feet. The creature had heard him. Jake scrambled over the wall and started to run, praying all the time that he could reach his car before Brad and the creature came after him.

Brad looked up when the panther gave the guttural cry. He heard someone moving away from the wall. An intruder had been on top of the wall, spying on him. His pet had heard the intruder's fall.

Kill!

Jumping up from the ground, Brad snapped his fingers. The creature followed him as he started in the same direction taken by the prowler. Brad hoped the intruder was someone who could be eliminated easily, a drifter or a homeless person who would not be missed.

When Brad reached the corner of the wall, he climbed up to have a look. A shape rustled in the shadows, but it was too far away for him to see clearly. Brad jumped down again and raced along the adjacent section of the wall.

The creature loped along faithfully next to him. It feared for its master. The scent of trouble was on the wind.

Halfway down the wall, Brad heard a car door slam. Like a trained gymnast, he pulled himself to the top of the barrier. A car engine chugged to life. Jake Taylor's green Chevy ran under a streetlight as it barreled away from Rocky Bank Estates.

A sharp pain creased Brad's skull making him dizzy. Jake had seen him on Alice's grave. He lost his balance, falling from the wall, blacking out for a moment. When he opened his eyes, the creature was licking his face.

Brad got up quickly. The evil voices were already buzzing inside him, calling for Jake Taylor's head. Jake knew Brad's secret, or at least part of it. And he would surely try to tell Cassie what he knew. Jake would take Cassie away, just as Alice had been taken away.

Brad flinched as the pain returned to his head. He saw the lifeless shape of Alice Gilbert lying in front of him with blood pouring from her mouth. Then the shadow appeared over his shoulder, falling on Alice's body. Brad turned but there was no one there. No memory beyond the shadow.

The creature rubbed against his legs. Sweat poured from his body. He remembered Cassie's sweet face. She was everything to him. She had to be protected from Jake Taylor.

But how could he get away with Jake's murder? He had to think out his plan, make it perfect. Killing Jake would be easy; getting away with the killing was something else entirely. He had to go into the house and sort it out.

As Brad turned toward the mansion, the pain

spread down into his neck. He heard Alice Gilbert's voice drifting across the misty grounds from the grove of trees. Brad didn't want to hear Alice anymore. He needed the evil voices if he was going to eliminate the enemy.

But Alice wouldn't leave him alone.

No, Brad, that's not what I want.

"Shut up! Just shut up!"

Please, Brad, don't hurt anyone else.

"No, Alice, get out of my head."

Please, Brad.

He started running toward the house to get away from her. The creature followed closely, still sniffing the air for danger. The night didn't seem to provide comfort for them anymore. Things would not be right again until Jake Taylor was gone.

Jake moved slowly in the swirling mists of the alley. He had parked the Chevy a few blocks from Cassie's house. He had to try one more time to warn her, even if she didn't want to listen.

He stared up at the second story, not sure which bedroom window belonged to her. A dim light burned in one of the rooms. Jake could see shadows moving on the wall. He could see a globe on top of a bookcase and assumed it was Cassie's room.

Jake picked up a pebble from the alley and tossed it against the window. He had to throw three pebbles before he got a response.

Cassie opened the window and looked out. "Brad, is that you?"

"No, it's me—Jake!"

A silence fell over the foggy alley for a moment.

"Cassie, listen to me."

"Go away, Jake."

Jake's voice was quavering. "Cassie, please listen to me. Brad's a psycho. He's got this strange animal out there at the estate. They were running around together. Brad was wallowing on the ground."

"What are you doing spying on him?" Cassie demanded. "Go home before you end up behind bars."

"Cassie, please. He's going to do something bad. I know it."

Cassie's eyes narrowed. She believed that Jake had finally lost his mind. How else could he make such unfounded accusations?

"Jake, go home now and I'll forget you came here."

"Cassie—"

"I mean it, Jake. You go home or I'll call the police."

She closed the window and turned off her light.

Chapter 10

Jake Taylor spent the next three weeks dodging his own shadow. He'd been spooked by the scene at the Forester estate. He froze every time he saw Brad in the hall at school. Jake was even more horrified to see Cassie always on Brad's arm. When they passed him in the hall, Brad and Cassie just ignored Jake, as if he had died or had committed some unpardonable sin.

The days were growing longer as prom time approached. Jake knew Cassie was going with Brad. They had been nominated Most Popular Junior Couple. The results of the voting would be announced at the prom.

Jake still feared for Cassie's safety. He had not hallucinated the creeping shadow of that sleek animal.

Yet nothing strange or threatening had happened since the day Brad had tried to run him over the cliff. Brad had been on his best behavior, which scared Jake even more.

Jake wondered if Brad might send the strange creature after him. He shuddered at the memory of the gliding behemoth in the trees. The animal's cry woke him from his sleep, sweat dripping from his face in the middle of the night.

Jake hadn't told anyone about the unusual occurrences at the Forester estate. He knew that no one would believe his story until he had absolute proof. After all, the Foresters were the pillars of Cresswell society, and it would take something strong to topple their disturbed son. But what? How could he possibly prove what a monster Brad was?

The Cresswell High Fine Arts Auditorium was festooned with crepe-paper streamers of blue and white, the school's colors. For the junior prom, the student council had hired a small orchestra, and a disc jockey for the more lively dances. Several rows of seats had been replaced by a portable hardwood dance floor that was erected in front of the stage.

A dark green curtain was drawn across the stage now. The orchestra and the disc jockey were quiet. Everyone had gathered in front of the stage for the Most Popular Couple announcement. The only junior who was not eagerly awaiting the crowning of the lucky couple was the lone figure who sat in the spotlight booth in the back of the auditorium.

The Friday before the prom, Mr. Lipton had asked Jake Taylor to run the spotlight for the evening. Jake had the responsibility of shining the beam on certain people during announcements and the spotlight dances. He also had to work the light for the announcement of the Most

Popular Couple. Since Brad and Cassie were among the nominees, Jake would have to shine the spotlight on them when they walked on stage.

Jake leaned back in his chair, sighing deeply. All night long he had been forced to watch Brad and Cassie as they danced together.

"Look alive, Taylor."

Jake almost fell out of the chair. "What the—?"

Mr. Lipton walked into the booth to check up on him. "The Most Popular Couple contest is coming up, Taylor. Are you going to be ready?"

Jake nodded. "Well, I guess I will."

"Don't get smart with me, kid."

"I've been doing all right so far, Mr. Lipton. But if you want to take over for me—"

"Just pay attention or you won't get your money."

Mr. Lipton left in a huff. Jake had wanted to turn down the job until he found out that it paid a hundred dollars for the night. Then he had rationalized that no one would see him in the booth. He could hide behind the spotlight and still keep an eye on Cassie.

A drum roll echoed through the auditorium. Jake sat up straight at the cue. He turned on the spotlight and aimed it at the president of the junior class, Bobby Pitlock. It was time to name the Most Popular Junior Couple.

As each couple paraded out onto the stage, Jake followed them with the spotlight. Finally Brad and Cassie came out. She looked so happy next to Brad.

The contestants all lined up together across the stage. Jake widened the spotlight beam for a moment. Bobby reached for the envelope that held the name of the winners. When the announcement was made, everyone gave a loud cheer. Jake lowered the beam, focusing on Brad Forester and Cassie Arthur, Cresswell High's Most Popular Junior Couple.

The band eased into a slow dance. Brad and Cassie had a spotlight dance on stage. Jake had to follow them with the bright circle, almost as if he were leading them around the stage. Tears stung his eyes.

When the dance was finished, Jake turned off the spotlight. His job was over for the evening. He wanted to go home to be alone for a while.

Jake locked up the booth and started for the stairs. As he approached the stairwell, he could hear Brad's voice. Brad and Cassie were standing on the stairs in an embrace. Jake fell back where they couldn't see him, listening to their conversation.

"You were great out there tonight," Brad said. "My shining angel."

Jake rolled his eyes, wondering how Cassie could fall for such slop.

"I can't believe it," Cassie replied. "We're really the Most Popular Junior Couple."

Jake cringed. He could hear them kissing. It was the perfect ending to an already horrendous night.

"Hey," Brad said, "let's get out of here."

Jake frowned.

"Why?" Cassie replied. "I'm having a great time."

"The dance is almost over," Brad said. "Mom and Dad wanted me to bring you to the house tonight. They have a surprise for you, a special party. You've never been to my house before."

"No, I haven't. I'll have to ask my mother first," Cassie said.

"Aw, come on. This is a special night. She won't care. I want to share something with you, Cassie. Something I've never shared with anyone."

"And your mother and father will be there?" Cassie asked.

"Yes, both of them. They really like you."

"All right," Cassie replied with a giggle. "Let's go."

Chapter 11

The red 280ZX swept through the patches of thin fog that hung over Rocky Bank Estates. Brad stared straight ahead with his hands on the wheel, guiding the car between the pockets of mist. The voices were silent inside him. He was heading for the moment of revelation, when he would be free of his pain and burden forever.

Cassie sat beside him in the car, leaning back with an innocent smile on her pretty face. She still could not believe that she and Brad had been named Most Popular Junior Couple. The whole school had recognized how good they were together by giving them a vote of confidence. Cassie wondered if things might get a little more serious. After all, Brad was taking her home for the first time to be with his family at the estate.

As they drew closer to the Forester mansion, Brad began to anticipate the lilting voice of Alice Gilbert. But Alice was silent now. Maybe the voices in his head would all go away now that he had Cassie's love. His salvation and his deliverance were at hand. Cassie would understand. She could free him from the suffering, forgive him for what he had done to Alice.

Cassie frowned when the car rolled into the long driveway of the Forester estate. The lights were dark inside the mansion.

"Brad, stop the car!"

Brad looked at her with an expression of disbelief. Cassie asked him again to stop. Brad finally braked the ZX, easing to a gradual halt.

"Cassie, what's wrong?"

Cassie peered at the dark house. "You said your parents would be home tonight. Are they here or not?"

Brad felt a sudden stabbing in the back of his neck. "They were going to be here but . . ."

"You lied to me," she said firmly. "Brad, you didn't have to do that."

Brad lowered his head, fighting the forces that had begun to stir inside him. "I wanted a special evening, Cassie, just you and me. My parents are gone for the weekend. I just thought we could spend some time alone. I was afraid you wouldn't come with me if you knew my parents weren't going to be here."

Cassie had a concerned expression on her face. "Brad, I don't now . . ."

He had never lied to her before. It was the first time he had done anything like this to Cassie. Now Brad seemed ashamed. He wouldn't look into her eyes.

"Don't you trust me, Cassie?" he asked in a penitent voice. "Have I ever given you any reason not to believe in me?"

"I'm sorry, Brad. It's just that, well, you've

never lied to me before. Why did you think you had to?"

"It's a white lie," Brad replied. "Like my dad says, the little white lies are necessary sometimes. I just wanted to surprise you."

Cassie sighed. "Well, I am surprised all right."

Brad started to turn the steering wheel, the final manipulation in the little scene he was playing. "I'm going to take you home, Cassie. I don't feel right, and I don't want to spoil this evening for you."

Cassie grabbed the steering wheel. "No. It's all right. I can stay for a little while, Brad, but I'd like your word that you'll take me home any time I ask."

"Sure, Cassie. I promise."

Brad felt a surge of energy through his body. Cassie wasn't going to be like Alice. She would understand when he revealed his innermost secrets.

Cassie touched his cheek with her fingertips. "You're so sweet, Brad. That's why we're Most Popular Junior Couple."

"Mr. and Mrs. Popularity," Brad replied.

The 280ZX started up the drive toward the mansion.

"The servants are off tonight," Brad said. "I'll give you the grand tour. We'll turn on every light in the house."

Cassie felt her heart beating inside her chest. She was a filled with a sudden foreboding. Something big was going to happen tonight. Cassie could just feel it.

"And now, for the next to the last stop on the tour!"

Brad flipped on a light in the huge kitchen of the mansion.

"Ta-da! For you, Cassie."

Her eyes grew wide. Brad gestured toward a table that was covered with heaping bouquets of red and white roses. The flowers had been strewn elegantly around the kitchen. In the middle of the flowers was a white cake with Cassie's name written in red icing. How could she have ever doubted her sweetheart?

"Brad, it's beautiful. I don't know what else to say."

She threw her arms around his neck, planting a kiss on his lips.

Brad broke off the kiss after a few seconds. "We're not finished yet. I've got something else for you."

He took a small, square, black box from the pocket of his tuxedo jacket. "This is for you, Cassie."

She hesitated. "What is it?"

"Go on, take it."

Cassie was breathless as she opened the box. Inside was a large, gold class ring from Cresswell High. Brad's initials were engraved on the inside band of the ring.

"It's beautiful," Cassie said.

"My father had it made for me a little early," Brad replied. "And I want you to wear it, Cassie. Will you?"

She nodded, almost speechless. "Yes."

They kissed for a long time. Brad embraced her tightly, hugging her close to him. It was time for him to introduce Cassie to his only other true friend.

He lifted her chin and looked deeply into her eyes. "Cassie, do you love me?"

She nodded. "Yes, I do, Brad."

"Cassie, there's someone else I'd like you to meet. A friend of mine."

Cassie looked around the kitchen. "Is he here now?"

"She," Brad replied. "Come on."

"She?"

Brad took Cassie's hand, guiding her toward the rear of the kitchen. She was becoming nervous as they emerged from the house into the misty, moonless night. Brad led her to another door on the side of the mansion.

"Brad, where are we going?"

"You'll see."

Brad was tingling inside. He had waited so long to share his secrets with someone who really loved him. His hand turned a key in the lock of the cellar door.

"Where are we going, Brad?"

"Try to be quiet," he said softly. "And don't make any sudden moves."

Cassie hesitated as Brad started down the basement steps. "Brad, it's so dark down here. Maybe you should take me home."

Brad ignored her. Instead, he flipped a switch,

and a dim bulb glowed in the stairwell. "No problem. There's plenty of light now."

She peered into the shadows. "Brad, who's down there?"

Brad shrugged. "My cat. I call her Alice. She has to be fed."

Cassie exhaled. "Cat? Why didn't you say so?"

"I didn't know if you liked cats."

"I love cats," Cassie replied.

Brad gripped her hand again tightly, leading her toward the basement. As Cassie descended the stairs, she noticed an awful odor emanating from the room below. But she still followed Brad under the eerie, incandescent light.

When the stepped into the dim basement, Cassie didn't see anything unusual. The room was set up like a workshop, complete with tools and a workbench along the wall. But then she heard the low, throaty growl from the deep shadows within.

"Brad!"

Cassie screamed as the panther loomed at them from the darkness. Black eyes reflected the dot of the single light bulb. The big jungle cat sprang straight at Brad.

Cassie was frozen. She expected the cat to claw Brad to death. Instead, the animal stood on its hind legs and put its paws on Brad's shoulders. It began to lick his face.

A shiver went through Cassie's body.

"Brad?"

He was rubbing the cat's long neck. "Isn't she beautiful, Cassie? Alice is a Florida panther, a rare black one. My father brought her to me last year. He found her on a hunting trip. Her mother was dead, so Dad brought her back from Florida. I raised her myself. Alice thinks I'm her mother."

Cassie's head was spinning. The stench in the basement made her nauseous. She wanted Brad to take her home immediately.

"Brad, listen to me!"

When she raised her voice at him, the panther growled at Cassie. She backed away, bumping into the workbench.

"What's wrong, Cassie?" Brad asked in a dry voice.

"I want to go home, Brad. Right now."

The cat growled again.

Brad smiled. "But I have so much more to tell you."

Cassie kept her eyes on the glassy stare of the big cat. "Please, Brad. You promised to take me home whenever I asked. I'm asking now."

Brad's eyes narrowed. "I think you're going to stay."

"No, Brad, that's not what I want."

He cringed, grabbing his forehead as the pain ripped through his skull. Alice had said the same thing before she rejected him. He heard the words again in his head.

No, Brad, that's not what I want.

"Stop it, Alice," he cried. "You aren't going to leave me. You—"

The little tramp.

Brad saw Alice's body as the shadow fell over

her. He turned but the figure was not there. The voice echoed in his tortured mind.

She had it coming.

Bury her, you fool.

No, Brad, that's not what I want.

Brad put his face in his hands. "Shut up! All of you shut up!"

The cat made another hostile sound.

Cassie started to inch her way toward the stairs. For a moment, she thought she was going to make it.

The cat growled at her. Cassie turned suddenly to run. She tripped on her heels, stumbling onto the stairs. The panther gave a vicious, shrieking cry. Cassie ran out of her shoes, hurrying up the stairs. Her heart was about to burst when she emerged into the night.

She raced for the grove of trees behind the mansion. Everything had turned sour so quickly. She wanted to wake from this nightmare and have Brad back again.

When she reached the trees, Cassie looked behind her. She couldn't see anyone running after her through the fog. Maybe Brad would leave her alone. She turned back to stare at the high stone wall. She had to climb over it and run to another house.

Suddenly something lunged at her from the darkness. The panther knocked her to the ground. It put its paws on Cassie's shoulders, pinning her to the damp earth above Alice Gilbert's grave.

Brad stood over her, a cruel look on his face. "I

thought you were different, Cassie. I thought you'd understand. But you're just like everyone else. You say you love me, but you really don't."

"Please, Brad!"

"Don't beg," he told her. "Have some dignity since you're going to die. You have to prepare yourself for death."

"Brad, don't hurt me."

He laughed hatefully. "I'm going to let you up now. But you better not scream or I'll have my friend rip out your throat."

Cassie trembled as she lifted herself from the ground. Brad dragged her back to the mansion where he tied her wrists and ankles and put a gag in her mouth.

After Brad had put the creature back in the cellar, he lifted Cassie over his shoulder. He carried her toward the garage. He needed a car with a trunk. Cassie was petrified as he lowered her into the dark trunk of his father's Coupe de Ville.

"Don't make a sound," Brad said.

He slammed the trunk shut, leaving Cassie in darkness. The voices were telling Brad to throw Cassie off the cliffs at Indian Point. He could claim that her death had been accidental, that she had lost her balance while they were walking. Everyone would believe his story. After all, he was the most popular boy at Cresswell High. His reputation was spotless. He could get away with anything.

Chapter 12

Cassie lay motionless in the car trunk, trying to breathe despite the suffocating darkness and the exhaust fumes. She could feel every bump and curve of the road as the Coupe de Ville hurried her toward her fate.

The car finally skidded to an abrupt halt. Cassie's body was aching from the ordeal. She listened for Brad over the idling engine.

Finally the trunk popped open and Brad appeared above her. He pulled her from the trunk and let her tumble to the hard ground.

Cassie whimpered behind the gag. She felt her wrists and ankles break free as Brad cut her loose. He jerked her to her feet and then pulled the gag from her mouth.

"Can't have you tied up," he told her in a hateful tone. "It has to look like we were taking a walk when you fell."

Cassie started to scream at the top of her lungs. Brad gave a hideous laugh. No one would hear her above the roar of the waves below.

Brad leaned closer to her, putting his lips against her ear. "Let's take a walk along the cliff. I had to stop where the guardrail was low so it could look like you really lost your balance and fell off."

"No, Brad, please don't—"

Brad started to pull her toward the cliff. Cassie's whole body felt weak and drained. Her legs wobbled beneath her, causing her to stagger as Brad dragged her toward the edge of the drop-off.

"You're going to fall," Brad whispered. He sounded as if he was having a good time. "The whole town will be talking about the tragic accident. I'll cry over your grave, and everyone will feel sorry for me. It'll work because everyone believes me."

Cassie heard the water lapping below. "No!"

A surge of adrenaline coursed through her body as they approached the ledge. Cassie began to fight him. She was not going willingly over the cliff.

Brad grabbed her wrists. "You could have had everything, Cassie. We could have been together forever. The perfect couple. The—Ow!"

Cassie kicked him in the shin, forcing Brad to let go of her. She started to run, but he caught her, knocking her to the ground. Brad pinned her to the walkway.

"You weren't satisfied," he said in a raspy voice. "You had to judge me, to think that I'm bad for what I did."

Brad climbed off her. Cassie started to crawl away, but Brad was right there again, pulling her to her feet. Cassie tried to hit him, to claw his face with her fingernails.

Brad caught her wrists again. "You wanted to leave me, and now you will—forever."

Cassie fought hard, kicking and screaming as he dragged her toward the cliff's edge. The voices were telling him to hurry, to get it over with. He could jump back into the running car and hurry to town to report what had happened. Cassie would pay for rejecting him, and he would get away with it.

"Please, Brad, I won't tell anyone. Just let me go. I promise I won't tell a soul."

She know's too much, kill her.

She had it coming.

The little tramp.

"Please, Brad—"

"You're going to die, Alice. You've got it coming, you little tramp."

Alice! Alice Gilbert? The girl who disappeared? Now Cassie understood. But was it too late?

She relaxed her body for a moment, pretending to faint. When Brad caught her in his arms, she quickly lifted her leg, slamming her knee into his groin. Brad buckled over, letting go of her.

Cassie staggered toward the idling car. If she could just get behind the wheel before Brad recovered, she would be able to get back into town before he could hurt her. She opened the car door, but a hand fell on her shoulder, stopping her from getting in.

Brad grabbed her in a bear hug and once again dragged her toward the edge of the cliff.

"No, Brad!"

She had it coming.
The little tramp.

They struggled at the edge of the cliff. Brad pulled her over the guardrail. But before he could throw her to her death, a pair of car headlights washed over them. Brad froze in the twin beams like a wild animal caught in the middle of a highway at night. Cassie screamed for help but Brad heaved her into the darkness.

Cassie reached out as she fell. Her fingers caught the lip of the rocky crag. She hung there with her legs dangling below her in the darkness. Brad lifted his foot to stomp on her fingers.

"No!" someone called out.

Suddenly Brad was no longer there. Cassie heard grunting and scuffling above her. Using the last strength in her arms, she lifted herself over the cliff. When she stood up behind the guardrail, she could see two figures struggling in front of the idling Coupe de Ville.

"Jake!" she screamed.

Brad swung a fist into Jake's stomach. Jake bent over, landing on his knees. Brad started back for the car.

Cassie picked up a heavy rock, rushing toward Brad. He was standing in front of the open car door when she lifted the rock over her head. He turned back to see the rock as she launched it toward him. Cassie missed, but by then it didn't matter.

To avoid the flying rock, Brad had to dive back into the front seat of the idling Coupe de Ville. As Brad fell, he reached out with his arm, accidentally hitting the gear shift. The car kicked into Drive.

Brad screamed as the car rolled forward. But there was nothing anyone could do to keep it from plowing through the guardrail. The Coupe de Ville plummeted toward the water, taking Brad along for the ride.

When the car tumbled off the cliff, Cassie screamed and put her hands over her face. Jake got up, staggering toward her, wrapping his arms around her shoulders. Cassie's body trembled as she laid her head on Jake's chest and sobbed. Jake stared down at the dark waters of Lighthouse Bay.

"It's okay," he said. "He's gone."

"I killed him," Cassie replied. "It was my fault."

Jake stroked her hair. "No, he killed himself. He got what he deserved. He was going to do the same to you."

Cassie broke away from him. "You've got to go down there, Jake. You've got to make sure."

Jake frowned. "I'm not climbing down those rocks. I could be killed myself."

"The state access road," Cassie replied. "It's not far away. It leads down to the shoreline."

"The place where the park service launches their boats?"

"We've got to try, Jake."

"Cassie, that's a dirt road. And it's not open to the public. Even if it was, I wouldn't want to drive down there in the dark."

"What if he's still alive?" Cassie asked.

"He'd never survive that fall."

Cassie peered into Jake's eyes. "What if he's alive and we could save him? We can't just let him die."

"He tried to kill us!"

She put her hand on his forearm. "We don't want to be like Brad, Jake."

Jake sighed. "All right," he said reluctantly. "Let's get it over with."

They raced back to the Chevy. Jake had been following Brad and Cassie since he had heard them talking at the prom. He had almost fainted when he saw Brad leave the estate alone in the Coupe de Ville. Jake thought that Brad had killed Cassie.

At the entrance to the access road, Jake had to get out to remove the cable that stretched across it. A sign declared, TRESPASSERS SUBJECT TO PROSECUTION. Jake guided the Chevy down to the water's edge.

"We shouldn't even be here," he said blankly.

"Please, Jake."

He was too stunned to argue. They left the headlights on as they got out of the car.

Cassie pointed out to the water. "There."

Whitecapped waves crashed against the dark monolith of the cliffs. But in the wash of the Chevy's headlights, Jake could see the tip of one car tire sticking up out of the water. The Coupe de Ville was almost completely submerged. He started wading into the cold waters of the bay, moving closer to the overturned vehicle.

The car had flipped, landing on its top. Brad

never could have survived the impact. The Coupe de Ville was squashed like a pancake.

Jake dived down and tried to open one of the doors, but it was no use. The doors and windows were all jammed shut. The roof had been pushed down to the steering wheel. Brad had to be dead if he was trapped inside.

Cassie saw Jake wading back toward her. "What did you find?" she called out.

Jake shook his head. He was soaked and shivering in the sea breeze. He limped back to the Chevy and turned on the heater. Cassie climbed in on the passenger side. Her face was pale and fretful. She looked wilted in the prom formal, which was torn and dirty from her fight with Brad.

"Let's go back to town," Jake said.

Cassie nodded. "This is a nightmare," she said in a daze. "We've just killed him."

Jake didn't waste any time backing the Chevy up the access road. He pulled back onto the main highway and got out to replace the cable across the entrance. When the cable was secure, they started toward Cresswell in silence.

"I always wanted to spend prom night with you," Jake said, "but I never imagined it like this."

"Jake, I'm sorry," Cassie replied. "You were right all along."

"Forget it," Jake replied. "Brad was pretty convincing. But it's over now."

"What are we going to do, Jake? Brad is dead."

He shook his head. "I don't know."

Cassie turned toward him with tears in her eyes. "We've got to go to the sheriff, Jake. We've got to tell the truth."

Jake snorted. "Are you crazy?"

"We have to tell the truth, Jake."

"Brad got what he deserved," Jake replied. "When they find him, they'll think it was an accident."

"But the sheriff is going to ask me about him," Cassie replied. "I was with Brad all night. What do I say then?"

Jake thought about it for a moment. "All right. Just say that Brad took you home after your little party. You don't know what happened after that."

"I can't lie, Jake. I just can't. Besides, they'll find your tire tracks out there. You were at the cliffs. Wouldn't it be better to tell the truth now?"

Jake sighed defeatedly. "All right, Cassie. We'll go to the sheriff first thing in the morning."

"No," Cassie replied. "Right now."

Chapter 13

Sheriff Tommy Hagen got out of bed when his deputy told him that there had been a death that night. Hagen hurried into the office in civilian clothes, taking a seat behind his desk. The ruddy, red-haired law officer sat and listened to the improbable story told by the two trembling teenagers. It took them almost an hour to get the whole thing out in the open.

Jake leaned back when he was finished. He felt better after his confession. Telling the truth had also made Cassie a little calmer. She sighed and put her hands in her lap.

Sheriff Hagen shook his head. "Now, let me see if I have this straight: Brad Forester tried to kill both of you, but he rode off the cliff in his father's Coupe de Ville. And he's also got some kind of wild animal out there at the estate."

"A panther," Cassie said. "Brad told me his father brought it from Florida after he had been on a hunting trip."

Hagen whistled as if he had heard a tall tale. "I know last night was Cresswell High's prom. Are you pulling some kind of prank? I mean, did you lose a bet, have to come in here and tell me this stuff as part of a gag? Because I don't think it's funny."

"We're telling the truth," Jake insisted.

"Brad Forester is one of the finest young men in this town," the sheriff replied. "He's a good kid."

"That's his act," Jake said. "Brad fooled everyone. He has two sides to his personality. He set me on fire, he ran me off the road, he tried to throw Cassie off the cliff—"

"He deliberately ran over a dog," Cassie said sadly.

"We're telling the truth, Sheriff Hagen."

The officer squinted at Jake and Cassie. "Okay," he said finally, "I'll have my men check it out. You two go home."

"No," Cassie replied. "I want to stay here."

Hagen sighed. "You two haven't told your parents about this, have you?"

"I called my mother on the way over," Cassie said. "She's very upset, but she believes me."

Hagen grimaced. "All right. We'll wait until my men have a look before we stir things up. I don't want to make trouble for anyone if we can avoid it."

"We're telling the truth," Jake said again.

The sheriff's eyes narrowed. "For your sake, Mr. Taylor, I hope you are."

Cassie saw Brad in front of her. His face had charged out of the darkness, looming toward her like a death mask. Cassie felt his hands on her shoulders. Brad was holding her down, trying to drown her beneath the surface of the black bay.

Cassie cried out in her sleep. She opened her eyes to see someone standing over her. His hands were on her shoulders, and he was trying to shake her back to consciousness. Cassie had fallen asleep on the couch in the sheriff's private office.

"Jake? Is everything all right?"

"The sheriff's back," Jake replied. "I think they found something out at the bay."

Cassie sat up, relieved to have escaped the horrible dream. She looked at the clock. It was almost six A.M. on Sunday morning.

The sheriff came back into the office, taking his place behind the desk. Jake and Cassie sat down in the seats opposite Hagen.

Sheriff Hagen had a strange expression on his face. "You two told some real whoppers, didn't you, Taylor?"

Jake's eyes grew wide with disbelief. "What?"

The sheriff leaned back in his chair. "My men went out to the cliffs, but they didn't find any Coupe de Ville."

"But it has to be there," Cassie replied. "Jake and I saw it."

Hagen shook his head. "They went all the way down to the end of the access road, but they didn't find a thing. We even sent a diver to look on the bottom of the bay, but he didn't see anything."

Jake sat on the edge of the chair, the old helpless feeling coming back to him. "That's impossible, sir. Brad went off that cliff. He crashed through the guardrail and hit the bay."

"The guardrail was broken," the sheriff replied. "And there were tire tracks. Some of the tracks belonged to your car, Taylor."

Jake couldn't believe what he was hearing. "I told you, I followed Brad and Cassie because I was afraid he would do something to her."

"What about Brad's body?" Cassie practically shouted. "Did you find it?"

"We dragged the bay," Hagen replied, "but nothing has turned up yet."

A shiver spread through Cassie's body. "He's doing it again. He's fooling everyone and he isn't even alive."

"We saw him go over the cliff," Jake exclaimed. "The car smashed on its top. It couldn't have been more than a hundred feet away from the shore."

Hagen focused his eyes on Jake. "Let's talk about your tire tracks, Taylor. You're behind all this nonsense, aren't you?"

"I told you, I was following Brad and Cassie." "Why?"

"Because I knew Brad was crazy!" Jake replied.

Hagen shifted in his chair. "You know, Taylor, one of my deputies told me that you almost went off a cliff yourself a while back. Brad Forester tried to help you, but you accused him of running you off the road."

"He did!" Jake said. "Then he tried to make it look like I was the one who lost control. You've got to believe us. We're telling the truth."

The sheriff turned his accusing eyes on Cassie. "Miss Arthur, you are Brad's girlfriend. If what you say is true, why didn't you suspect something before tonight?"

Cassie lowered her eyes. "He had me fooled. It was all an act. Brad was good at fooling people."

Hagen leaned forward, folding his hands on the desk. "I'm sending you home," he said. "And I'm also calling your parents to tell them that you wasted my time coming here with all this hogwash."

Jake pointed toward the door. "Go out to the Forester estate. Get a warrant and search the place. You'll find Brad's little pet in the basement."

"I've already called the Forester estate," the sheriff replied. "A maid told me that Brad had gone away to join his parents for the rest of the weekend."

"Impossible!" Jake cried. "I'm telling you the truth. Brad went off the cliff in that car."

Cassie sat up straight in her chair, focusing her brown eyes on the law officer. "Sheriff, there's something I have to tell you. I think Brad had something to do with the disappearance of Alice Gilbert."

"That's not funny, young lady!"

Cassie was unfazed by his disbelief. "Brad kept calling me Alice after he lost his mind. And Alice is the name of that panther he keeps at the estate."

Hagen stood up behind his desk. "Miss Arthur, I'm not making trouble for the Forester family. Is that clear? When you leave this office, we're going to forget all about your visit, except for my calling your parents."

Jake and Cassie just sat there, wooden and numbed. They couldn't believe that the sheriff's deputies had failed to find the Coupe de Ville or Brad's body.

Hagen cleared his throat. "I'm sending you two home," he said in a gruff voice. "Now get out of here and don't let me see your faces in this office again."

Jake and Cassie walked out of the station. In the light of day, the whole thing seemed like a bad dream.

"You want to go home?" Jake asked.

Cassie nodded. "We're going to be in trouble."

"You see what it's been like for me," Jake said. "Even when we think we've killed Brad in self-defense, nobody believes us."

"Oh, Jake." Cassie threw her arms around him, sobbing. "I'm so sorry I treated you badly."

"It's okay," he replied. "I'll drive you home."

Jake started the Chevy, and they chugged home toward the Upper Basin. He wondered how long it would be before the body of Brad Forester floated to the surface of Lighthouse Bay.

When Cassie walked into the house, her mother was waiting for her. Mrs. Arthur was dressed in her church clothes. It was almost time for her to leave to go teach her Sunday school class.

"Cassie, are you all right?"

Cassie was so drained that she couldn't cry anymore. "I don't want to talk right now, Mom. I can't."

Mrs. Arthur seemed more concerned than angry. "I just spoke to the Sheriff. He said they didn't find the car or the body, and he was very upset that you should play a prank like this. Cassie, what's going on?"

Cassie sighed. "I know what I saw, Mom. It's just as I explained to you last night. Brad tried to kill me. Then, when I was about to throw a rock at him, he went over the cliff in his car."

Mrs. Arthur put her hands on Cassie's shoulders. "I trust you, honey. I have to go to church now. I was going to go to Porterville after church to see your Aunt Martha, but I think I better come back here to be with you."

Cassie drew away from her mother. "It's all right, Mom."

"Do you want to go to church with me?"

"I'll go next week," Cassie replied. "I feel sick."

"Cassie—"

"Please, Mom. Go to Aunt Martha's. Please. I can take care of Andrea. Where is she anyway?"

"She slept over at Stephanie's," Mrs. Arthur replied. "She's going to spend the day there after church. Stephanie's mother will drive her home after dinner."

Cassie nodded absently. She had told the truth. What else could she do if no one believed her? She just wanted to sleep, to let go of everything for a few hours.

"I'll be fine, Mom."

Mrs. Arthur hugged her daughter again. "I trust you, Cassie. You're a good girl. I'll be home by eight or nine, I promise."

Cassie thanked her mother and staggered toward her room. She used her last bit of energy to climb the stairs. She didn't even bother to change out of her tattered gown before she fell into bed.

As soon as her eyes were closed, Cassie drifted into a long, fitful slumber. She began to dream of the dark waves that washed across the bay and over the body of Brad Forester. Brad floated toward her with the death mask drawn tightly across his face.

Cassie cried out, waking from the nightmare. She sat up in her bed. Something moved to her left, heading for the window.

She peered toward the open window in the first shadows of twilight. She had slept all day and now woke to find a black shape hanging in the window frame. The figure perched there for a moment like a gargoyle on top of a castle.

"Who's there?"

"Cassie."

The familiar voice filled her room. Something hit her in the chest. Cassie blinked and the figure in the window was no longer there.

Reaching to her right, she switched on the lamp next to her bed. The object that had hit her chest was now lying in her lap. Cassie's whole body began to shake when she lifted the object into the light.

"Oh, no!"

Climbing out of bed she hurried downstairs,

turning on every light in the living room. Her mother hadn't come home yet, and Andrea was still at her friend's house. Cassie was all alone.

Picking up the phone, she quickly dialed Jake's number. "Jake, it's Cassie. You've got to come over right now. Brad's alive."

"How do you know?" he asked.

"Because I just woke up with Alice Gilbert's diary on my chest."

Cassie waited in the living room for Jake to arrive. In her hands she clutched the pink diary that had once belonged to Alice Gilbert. Alice's name was written in a neat, fluid script at the bottom of the front cover. Next to that, in smaller but equally precise penmanship, was her address in Gaspee Farms. Cassie's suspicions about Brad and Alice were now confirmed.

Cassie couldn't believe that Brad was really alive, that he had somehow survived the fall over the cliff. But it must be true. Some miracle must have spared him from being crushed in the twisted metal of the Coupe de Ville.

Cassie looked down at the dirt-smudged cover of the diary. If Brad wasn't alive, maybe he had an accomplice in all of his hateful undertakings. It would make more sense than explaining how Brad's dead body had climbed out of its watery grave to terrorize her again.

She started to open the diary, but she was startled by a sound outside. Cassie held her breath as someone rapped sharply on the door.

"Cassie?"

"Jake, thank God."

She threw her arms around him as soon as he was inside. "I'm so glad to see you. You got here quickly."

"Cassie, what's wrong? You're shaking like a leaf. And what's all this about Brad?"

She drew back, looking into his eyes. "Jake, Brad was here. I heard him call my name. He climbed through my window and left this." She handed him the diary.

Jake's eyes grew wide. "Alice Gilbert's diary. Unbelievable!"

"I'm scared, Jake."

They sat down on the sofa and began to read.

Jake shook his head and whistled. "Alice was secretly dating Brad all right. She mentions him by name. Listen: 'Have to break off with Brad. I love him but *he* is a problem.' She underlined the word *he*. I wonder why."

Cassie pointed to another passage. "Here. 'I love Brad but something is not right. *He* bothers me. I don't feel comfortable with *him*.' She keeps underlining the same words, *he* and *him*. And look. The last entry was made only two days before she disappeared."

Jake read it aloud. " 'Going to break up with Brad. It's final.' It sure was final. Too final."

Cassie looked away, leaning back on the sofa. "Brad was trying to kill me. I bet he killed Alice."

"She could still be alive," Jake offered. "She disappeared, but no trace of her was found."

A shiver ran like a cold draft over Cassie's

shoulders. "He's alive, Jake. I can feel it. Brad is alive."

Jake frowned, closing the diary. "How could he have survived that fall? Even Brad couldn't pull that one off?"

"No?" Cassie replied. "How many times did he pull things off and no one suspected? How many times did he fool everyone?"

Jack sighed. "I see what you mean. He—"

Cassie put her hand on his forearm. "Shh. Listen!"

Again footsteps sounded on the front porch. They peered toward the front door. The knob turned and the door began to creak open.

"Hi, Cassie!"

Andrea pushed into the living room, home from her stay at her friend's house.

Cassie got up and ran to her sister, putting her arms around her. "I'm so glad you're home, Andrea."

"You're going to get in trouble, Cassie. You aren't supposed to have boys over when Mom's not here. You're breaking the rules."

"Hi, Andrea," Jake said. They knew each other by sight, but this was the first time they had met.

"Hi," the girl answered sheepishly.

Cassie directed Andrea toward the stairs. "Go up to your room right now. Close the door and make sure you lock it."

Andrea suddenly seemed frightened. "What's wrong?"

"Nothing," Cassie replied. "Mom will be home

soon. You just go wait in your room. Everything will be all right."

Andrea hurried up the stairs and locked herself in her room. Cassie felt bad about having to frighten her, but she wanted Andrea to be safe. There was no need to involve her in any of the trouble.

Jake was still on the sofa, staring at the diary. "This is too weird, Cassie. What's going on?"

Cassie sat down beside him. "Jake, we've got to go back to the sheriff."

Jake shook his head. "What's it going to look like when we go into Hagen's office with this diary and say that Brad left it for you? What's it going to look like when Brad's body washes up in the bay?"

"He's not dead," Cassie insisted. "I know it."

"We'll look like fools. The sheriff will think it's another prank. We'll be lucky if they don't lock us up."

Cassie grabbed the diary from him. "We have this! It's something."

Jake shook his head. "That will only get us arrested. They'll accuse me of having something to do with Alice's disappearance."

Cassie looked down at the floor. "I know Alice is somewhere on that estate. That animal probably killed her. Brad buried her in those trees where you saw him wallowing in the dirt. The sheriff could get a warrant. He could search the place."

"He wouldn't do it before," Jake replied. "What makes you think he'll do it now? Brad's father is too powerful. Even if Hagen wanted to search the estate, Mr. Forester would get out of it somehow. People like that always do."

Cassie clenched her fists. "What else can we do?"

She turned to look at Jake. Their eyes met for a moment. They sat there looking at each other as if for the first time. He was about to kiss her when all of the lights went out, leaving the living room pitch-black.

"He's back!" Cassie whispered in the darkness.

Jake stood up, trying to get his bearings. "It's probably just a fuse. You had every light turned on. It's just an overload. Where's the fuse box?"

"In the basement."

"Stay here," Jake said. "I'll go check it."

"No way," Cassie replied. "I'm going with you."

Cassie's mother kept a flashlight at the top of the basement stairs for just such emergencies. They crept slowly down the stairs, sinking into the cool, musty air of the basement. Jake swung the beam of the flashlight until he saw the fuse box on the wall.

"Somebody loosened the main fuse," Jake said. "Here."

He tightened the fuse and the lights glowed again upstairs. They could see the incandescence spilling into the basement through the door. They could also hear the screams that suddenly sounded from the second floor.

"Andrea!" Cassie cried.

She ran up the basement stairs with Jake behind her. Andrea continued to scream as they hit the stairs to the second floor. Cassie tried the door to Andrea's room, but it was locked. Andrea's cries stopped abruptly and the house was quiet.

"Andrea!"

Jake shoved Cassie aside and pounded his shoulder into the door. He broke through on the third try. But it was too late. The window was open and Andrea was no longer in the bedroom.

"He took her!" Cassie cried.

They heard a car engine racing in the alley behind the house. Jake stuck his head out of the window in time to see a flash of red under a streetlight as the car turned onto the street. Jake had seen the car before.

"Brad!"

Cassie was trembling. "No, it can't be. He's got her. He's got my sister. Brad is going to kill Andrea."

Then she spotted something over Jake's left shoulder. "What's that?"

Jake turned to see a lavender dress hanging from the curtain rod. Another present had been left for them. Cassie walked toward the dress, touching the lacy hem.

"I know this dress," she said.

"What is it?"

Cassie studied the garment closely. "I think it's the dress that Alice Gilbert was wearing when she disappeared. I remember the description."

"Are you sure?" Jake asked.

Cassie nodded blankly. "Yes, lavender with

lace. She used to wear this dress to the honor society meetings."

"He's trying to frame us," Jake said. "Somehow he survived that fall, and he's trying to pin Alice's disappearance on us."

"He can't get away with this."

"He's crazy," Jake replied. "He's setting us up in a big way."

Cassie looked horrified. "Jake, he's got Andrea."

"We've got to stop him before he hurts her!" Jake exclaimed. "We've got to hurry."

Cassie shook her head. "No, we've got to go to the sheriff. He can get Andrea back."

Jake grabbed her arms, turning her toward him. "They'll never believe us, Cassie! Hagen will never get a warrant to search the Forester estate!"

"We can take the diary to them," Cassie replied. "And the dress. They'll have to believe us then."

"No, Cassie. It won't work. They'll think it's another prank. Hagen isn't going to listen to us a second time."

She broke away from him. "What do you think we should do?" she asked quietly.

"He took Andrea in order to lure us out to the estate," Jake said. "We have to go out there and save her. But we can't fall into any trap Brad may have set for us. We have to be smarter than he is. We have to beat him at his own game."

She saw him staring at the lavender dress. His

eyes were wide. Jake took the dress from the hanger.

"I have a plan, Cassie, but you've got to help me."

He held the dress against her body.

"What are you doing, Jake?"

"If Brad's still alive, we can sink him, Cassie."

"I'm afraid, Jake. Really afraid."

"Trust me, Cassie. It's the only way."

The plan was forming quickly in Jake's mind. He could beat Brad at his own game, if Brad had indeed survived the fall from the cliff. They would head for the Forester mansion as soon as Jake had stopped at his own house to retrieve his father's gun from the steamer trunk in the attic.

A half hour later, Jake and Cassie were standing on the roof of the green Chevy, peering through the lowland fog that had settled over the Forester estate. Jake had driven around to the back of the estate, parking next to the stone wall. They could barely see beyond the grove of trees where Brad and the panther had captured Cassie. Her skin crawled when she gazed down at the unholy place.

Jake studied the swirling mists. He could see the looming shape of the mansion beyond the trees. There didn't seem to be any lights on in the house. It appeared that Brad's parents had not come home yet. A ghostly silence had settled in with the fog.

"I don't see anyone," Jake said to Cassie.

Cassie was having second thoughts, especially

since she had seen the gun tucked into Jake's belt. "Maybe we should go to the sheriff."

Jake grimaced. "Your sister is in there, Cassie. We have to do it just like we planned. It's the only way."

Cassie took a deep breath. The damp air seemed to cling to her skin, making her feel clammy all over. She knew Jake was right. They had to move quickly to rescue Andrea before she was hurt.

"That cat is still around here somewhere," Jake said. "I'll have to kill it. I just hope Dad's gun will bring it down."

Cassie turned away from the wall, leaning back against the stone. "I hope we're doing the right thing, Jake."

He looked at Cassie. "What else can we do?"

"I know, I know, you're right."

"Just remember how we planned it, Cassie. If we pull it off, Andrea will be fine and we'll finally nail Brad."

"I just hope he hasn't hurt her," Cassie replied. "Jake, what if we're dealing with some kind of ghost? What if Brad really did come back from the dead?"

Jake peered over the wall again. "There's no such thing as ghosts, Cassie. Come on. Let's go over the top."

Cassie grabbed his arm, squeezing tightly, trying to give herself courage.

"All right!" she said. "All right."

She took a deep breath, bracing herself for the worst. The whole thing had been a nightmare.

Why couldn't she wake up in her own bed and have things the way they were before?

"Here," Jake said. "I'll give you a boost up."

Cassie hoisted herself to the top of the wall and looked toward the dark mansion, which was hidden in the mist. Jake climbed up next to her.

"I'll go down first," he said.

He jumped to the ground and then called to her. Cassie swung her legs over, dangling from the wall. For a moment she felt as if she were going to fall, but Jake grabbed her legs and helped her the rest of the way.

They moved in the fog, crouching behind the cover of a large oak tree. Their eyes studied the swirling mist. Was Brad really out there somewhere with his horrendous pet? Did he really have Andrea and was he planning to do her harm?

They moved to within a hundred yards of the mansion. "I'm going in," Jake said.

"Jake—"

He took her hand. "Just remember how we planned it. If things don't work out, run for help."

He started to move away from her.

Cassie grabbed his arm.

"It's okay," he replied. "I'm ready."

He held up the pistol.

She pulled him closer to her, kissing him lightly on the cheek.

Jake blushed and patted her hand. "We're going to get your sister out of here, Cassie. I promise."

"Be careful."

Cassie watched as Jake began to tiptoe through the fog. He disappeared as the cloud of mist swirled around him. Cassie leaned back against the tree, looking for signs of danger in the still night.

Her heart fluttered as something began to move toward her, scuttering between the tree trunks. Cassie's eyes grew wide as the noise came closer to her. She expected the black panther to leap at her from the night.

Instead a harmless rabbit hopped past her, stopping for a moment to look at the brown-haired girl in the lavender dress. Cassie let out a sigh of relief. The rabbit hopped off into the bushes. The real trouble wouldn't come until she heard the commotion echoing from the mansion.

As Jake moved slowly through the fog, his feet made a squeaking noise on the wet grass. He stopped, rubbing his face with the back of his hand. When he looked up again, he could see the dark edge of the mansion in the mist.

Jake wondered if Brad really could still be alive. He had seen Brad pull off other stunts that were hard to believe. But coming back from the dead was the ultimate ruse. Even if he was alive, had he really taken Andrea?

Jake had to keep going forward. Andrea might still be alive. If she was, Jake and Cassie were her only chance, especially if Brad was planning to feed her to that panther.

The gun felt heavy in Jake's hand as he drew closer to the kitchen at the rear of the house. His whole body was weak, almost trembling. He wasn't sure he could shoot Brad or anyone else, even in self-defense. His finger was loose on the trigger of the thirty-eight as he stepped up beside the kitchen window.

The kitchen was completely dark. There didn't seem to be anyone around, not even servants. Hadn't Sheriff Hagen talked to a maid when he called the mansion? Maybe that was another one of Brad's tricks.

Jake started for the cellar door on the side of the house. He had seen Brad come out of the cellar with the panther. Jake found the door and tried the knob. The door was unlocked.

Holding his breath, Jake slowly opened the door. He peered down into the shadows of the stairwell. He couldn't see or hear anything. The mansion seemed to have been abandoned.

Jake moved back from the door, turning to stare toward the trees. What if Brad had taken Andrea someplace else? Suddenly his plan seemed ridiculous. Cassie had been right. They should have gone straight to the sheriff. After all, Andrea had been kidnapped, a fact that even Hagen would have trouble disputing.

Jake began to retreat. But, suddenly a light came on in the stairwell. Jake stopped cold, exposed in the dim glow of the single bulb. He wasn't sure what to do until he heard the high, piercing sound of Andrea's screams.

Jake lifted the thirty-eight in front of him, creeping slowly toward the dim light of the stairs. He peered down into the hollow of the stairwell.

Shapes danced on the wall like the puppets of a shadow play. He flinched when he heard Andrea scream again.

At least she was still alive. But for how long? Thumbing back the hammer of the pistol, he started down the stairs, taking each step cautiously.

Andrea's desperate voice rose again, only this time her words were clearer. "No, keep it away! Keep it away!"

The cat's cry came after Andrea's voice, rising in the stairwell like something from hell. Jake clomped down the stairs, leaping into the basement. His eyes grew wide when he saw the panther snarling in the face of the blond-haired girl.

"Andrea!"

Her pitiful face lifted into the dull light. "Jake! Help me! It's going to hurt me!"

The panther was tethered to the wall with a short length of chain that held it only inches away from Andrea. The poor girl was tied up, unable to move away from the beast.

"Jake!"

"Andrea, stay still."

"Help me, Jake. Please."

"I will, Andrea. I will."

The light was bad in the cellar. Jake hung back in the doorway, peering toward the frantic beast. The panther had begun to move back and forth, its black eyes focused on Jake. He lifted the pistol, steadying his aim with both hands. It would be a hard shot in the semidarkness.

"Jake, hurry!"

He had to lower the gun for a moment to wipe the sweat from his eyes. When he looked back into the shadows again, the cat was frozen on its belly, growling as if it knew that Jake meant it harm. Something inside Jake made him wish he didn't have to shoot the poor creature. It had been taken from its home and raised to obey a monster. The panther didn't really deserve to die.

"Jake, please!"

But he had to save Andrea, and that meant killing the cat. He raised the gun again, sighting the panther the way his father had taught him. Put the front bead of the pistol in the notch of the rear sight. Squeeze the trigger slowly so the shot would go true. He hoped to hit the animal in the chest, maybe put the slug through its heart.

"This is it," he muttered to himself.

The animal was in the sight. Jake squeezed the trigger, but the panther didn't die. Just as he fired the gun, someone swung at him from the side, hitting his wrist with a broom handle. The thirty-eight went off as Jake dropped it to the floor. The shot didn't hurt anyone, but the noise was deafening and the smoke swirled opaquely in the confines of the basement.

Someone fell on top of Jake, knocking him to the floor. He tried to get up, but the cold barrel of the pistol was suddenly pressed against the back of his neck. Brad told him not to move or he would blow his brains out.

* * *

Cassie cringed against the tree trunk when she heard the pistol erupt in the night. The echo reverberated in the fog, rolling over the grounds toward Cresswell. There was only one gunshot, making her wonder if Jake had killed Brad or the panther.

She wasn't sure what to do next. Peering around the side of the tree, she could see only the fog and the vague outlines of the mansion. The gunshot had seemed muffled, as if it had come from inside the house. But there were still no lights burning in any of the windows.

Jake had asked Cassie to go for help if something went wrong with their plan. What if Jake or Andrea was the one who had gotten hurt? Maybe Brad had done something to them.

Leaning back against the tree, she told herself to go for help. But she couldn't. She had come this far. She had to carry through with their plan to save her sister. She had to follow Jake in case he had gotten into trouble.

Standing up on wobbly legs, she moved from behind the tree, taking steps toward the mansion. As she emerged from the grove, she stopped, staring toward the dim glow that now appeared in the fog. She heard voices rising in the spectral mist. Cassie started forward again.

Jake gaped up at the bare-chested teenager who held his father's gun on him. "I don't believe it."

Brad's face was hidden in the shadows. He backed up until he was standing in the light. It was Brad all right, down to the horrible expression on his handsomely evil face.

"How did you survive that fall?" Jake asked.

Brad laughed triumphantly. "You little puke. Did you really think you could kill me? I'm invincible."

"You went off that cliff in the car."

"So what?" Brad replied. "I got lucky. When the car flipped, I was thrown clear. I landed out in the deep water. I'm the captain of the diving team, or had you forgotten?"

"How did you get the car out of the water?"

Brad smiled proudly. "After I swam to shore, the first car I saw was a twenty-four-hour tow truck. The driver was coming out to Indian Point to take his dinner break. I had to bribe him plenty to get the car out of the water and up the access road. But he did it for me, and I had him pull the car to a junkyard near Timberlake. Cool, huh?"

Jake shook his head. "Incredible."

Brad leaned over, shoving the barrel of the gun in his face. "I had to come back, you little jerk. I had to make you pay for stealing my girl. Now I can do whatever I want to you."

"Help!" Andrea cried.

The panther gave a shrill, jungle cry. It pulled tightly at the chain, trying to get at Jake. The beast could sense the danger from the boy who had brought the gun. It wanted to protect Brad from the intruder.

Brad fixed his gaze on the cat. "Down, Alice!"

The panther immediately dropped to its belly, keeping its black eyes focused on Jake.

"She does what I tell her," Brad said.

Jake kept his eyes on the gun. "Does it like it here in the basement, Brad?"

Brad swung the gun, hitting Jake in the face. "Her!" he cried. "Don't call her 'it.' She has a name. Alice. Go on, say it."

"Alice," Jake mumbled, rubbing his cheek.

Brad laughed maniacally. The evil voices were raging inside him. They were telling him to kill these two wimps. He had to eliminate anyone who could hurt him. He had to make Jake pay for taking Cassie away from him.

"Don't let her kill us," Jake pleaded. "You can get help, Brad. They won't be too tough on you if you let us live."

Brad lowered his head for a moment. "I killed Alice. They'll hurt me for that."

No, Brad, that's not what I want.

Kill.

The little tramp.

She had it coming.

Bury her, you fool.

Jake gazed up at the tormented face of his captor. "Brad—"

"Shut up! All of you, shut up!"

A pain streaked up Brad's neck, driving through his skull. Suddenly he was back in the half-light, standing over Alice Gilbert's body. Blood trickled from her dead mouth. The shadow appeared over her body, but when Brad turned to look, the figure was gone.

"Forester, listen to me," Jake implored.

Brad kicked Jake in the side. He had to kill him.

It was the only way to appease the voices inside his head. They were calling for blood. But Brad knew he still had to be slick so no one would suspect that the deaths of Andrea and Jake had been by foul play. The voices told him to go back to the cliffs.

"You can get help, Brad."

"Help! I don't need help. Not when you're going to steal my car, Taylor. You'll need help. All the help you can get—before you die."

"What?"

Brad nodded, leering at Jake. "You're going to steal my car, Taylor. Then you're going to kidnap Andrea and take her for a joyride. Only this time you're the one who'll go over the cliff."

"You can't!" Jake cried.

"Why not?"

"Because Cassie will tell what happened," Jake replied. "She'll go to Hagen and tell him everything."

Brad hesitated for a moment before he spoke. "Hagen will never believe her. Did he believe you the first time? Huh?"

Jake scowled at him. "You creep."

Brad waved the barrel of the pistol. "When Hagen called here, I had just gotten home. I disguised my voice to sound like the maid. It was great."

"You rotten creep."

"Did Hagen give you a hard time?" Brad asked.

"You'll never get away with this," Jake replied. "They'll find that cat. Somehow you'll get yours."

Brad reached down with his left hand, grasping the front of Jake's shirt. "They'll never find her. Hagen will never come on this property, with or without a warrant. He doesn't want to upset my father. Half of his men are on the take anyway."

"You'll have to kill Cassie, too," Jake said.

"I will if I have to," Brad replied. "Now get over there."

Brad pushed Jake toward the workbench. Jake watched as Brad quickly unleashed the big cat. On Brad's verbal command, the dark-eyed animal inched forward, trapping Jake against the workbench. The dim light bulb reflected from the primitive stare of the panther. Jake tried to turn sideways, but the animal cried out and showed its teeth.

Brad went back for the girl. He grabbed Andrea, untied her, and pulled her across the basement floor. Jake tensed but the animal kept him from helping the girl. Brad had the gun and the panther, leaving Jake little hope of getting out alive. He prayed that Cassie had heard the shot and that she had run for help.

Brad stopped with Andrea in front of him, waving the gun at the stairs. "You first, Taylor. And don't try to run. Alice will catch you if you do. She'll tear out your spine if I tell her to."

Jake started up the stairs with the panther following him on Brad's command. He could not escape the quickness of the big cat. Without the gun, he had no way to kill it. As he neared the top of the stairs, he could hear Brad behind him, pulling Andrea up the steps.

"Let me go!" the girl cried.

"Shut up, you little tramp."

Jake emerged from the basement into the mist. He gaped at the slender figure before him. The cat started to growl at the lavender vision in the fog-diffused light. A halo seemed to surround the delicate female form. Cassie started to speak, but Jake waved her off.

Brad stopped dead when he came through the door with Andrea in front of him. His eyes grew wide at the luminous figure in the swirling mist. In the lavender dress, Cassie's resemblance to Alice Gilbert was uncanny. She stretched out her arms toward Brad.

Brad's lips began to tremble. "Alice?"

Cassie looked quickly to Jake, who nodded. Brad seemed to be confused.

"Alice, is that really you?"

"Yes, Brad," Cassie replied. "It's me. And I've come back to help you make everything right."

Brad just stood there, gawking at Cassie in the lavender dress. For a moment, Jake thought Brad would remember that he had left the dress at Cassie's house when he kidnapped Andrea. But Brad remained motionless, his mouth hanging open. The image of Alice Gilbert was too strong in his mind. Cassie's impersonation had mesmerized him.

"Hello, Brad," Cassie said again.

Brad shook his head. "Alice? But . . . you can't be alive. You can't."

Cassie struggled to keep her wits about her. "You're alive, Brad. You fell off the cliff and you're still here."

"Yes," Brad replied. "How did you know about that?"

"I know everything about you," Cassie replied.

"Alice," Brad repeated. "You're so beautiful."

Jake clenched his fists, watching Brad carefully. The trick was working. Brad couldn't tear his eyes away from the lavender apparition. He let go of Andrea, who immediately started to run toward Cassie.

Jake grabbed Andrea, restraining her. "No," he whispered. "Leave her alone. Brad is about to give up."

Andrea stopped squirming and pointed toward Cassie. "But that's my sis—"

Jake wrapped his hand over her mouth. "Hush. Brad has to believe that Cassie is Alice Gilbert. Our lives depend on it."

Cassie held out her arms to Brad. "All is forgiven, my love. You're safe now. No one can hurt you."

Brad staggered toward her, holding the gun loosely in his hand. "But I killed you, Alice. You're dead."

Cassie smiled. "No, I'm here. I'm alive, Brad. I want you to drop the gun."

Brad closed his eyes, swaying back and forth for a moment. Jake thought about jumping him, but Brad still held the thirty-eight. And the big cat was right there beside its master.

"I won't hurt you," Cassie said, taking a step toward Brad.

The panther growled and tensed. It didn't seem to be fooled by the lavender illusion. Its dark nose still detected the scent of danger in the air.

Cassie frowned and stepped backward, keeping her eye on the cat. "Don't let it hurt me, Brad."

Brad threw a look at the cat. "Down, Alice. Down!"

The cat hesitated before it obeyed the command.

Cassie put a hand to her throat, staring at the animal. "You called it Alice."

Brad smiled. "I named her after you, honey. Isn't she beautiful? Dad brought her to me last year after I . . ." The smile disappeared and his face went slack again.

"What's wrong?" Cassie asked cautiously.

"I hurt you," Brad replied. "I killed you."

Cassie tried to smile warmly. "No, Brad, you never hurt me. And I'm here to help you make everything all right."

Cassie stole a quick look at Jake and Andrea. Jake motioned, pointing at the gun. Cassie knew what to do, but she had to take it slow, even if Brad was beginning to trust her. His face was like a happy child's. He looked as if Alice Gilbert's reappearance had washed away his burdens.

Brad pointed toward the mansion. "Alice, I want to show you something. It's in my room."

Cassie fixed her gaze on the gun. "I'll go with you, Brad, but you should give Jake the pistol."

Brad seemed confused. "Jake?"

"Yes," Cassie replied, "Jake. The gun belongs to him. You should give it to him before we go up to your room."

Brad shook his head like a petulant child. "No, I won't do it."

"Please," Cassie said. "Do it for me, Brad. Then we can go up to your room. Everything will be fine."

He stared dreamily into her eyes. "For you?"

"I'd really appreciate it," Cassie said.

"All right, Alice. I'll do it for you."

"Thank you, Brad."

Brad held out the gun to Jake, telling him to take it. Jake started slowly toward Brad, reaching for the thirty-eight. But the panther got up to come between Jake and its master. Jake saw the animal's bared teeth.

Cassie touched Brad's arm. "Don't let it hurt Jake," she said sweetly. "Please, Brad."

"Down!" Brad cried. "Down!"

The cat dropped on its back haunches, keeping its dark eyes focused on Jake.

"Now," Cassie urged, "give Jake the gun."

Brad's face softened when he looked at her again. "All right, Alice. Here, take it."

Jake took the gun from Brad's hand. He stepped back next to Andrea, holding the weapon on Brad. But Brad didn't notice that there was a gun pointed at him. He was gazing with adoration at Cassie.

"There," he said. "I did it, Alice."

"Thank you, Brad."

Andrea tried to start toward her sister again. Jake tightened his arm around her, whispering that they had to keep pretending Cassie was Alice Gilbert until the sheriff got there. They weren't through yet.

Brad took Cassie's hand. "Let's go up to my room."

Cassie gently shook her head. "No, Brad. Let's stay here for a while."

She looked at Jake, who pointed toward the cellar and then nodded in the direction of the cat. Cassie understood perfectly. They had to get the beast under lock and key before they were completely safe again.

"What about Alice?" Cassie said to Brad.

Brad smiled weakly. "But you're Alice."

"No, your wonderful, lovely panther," Cassie replied dreamily. "Shouldn't we make sure she's safe before we go inside? We wouldn't want anything to happen to her."

Brad looked toward the cat. "Yes, you're right, Alice. I wouldn't want anything to happen to her."

Suddenly a pair of glaring floodlights flashed on in back of the mansion, blinding everyone for a moment. A car door slammed and a hulking figure emerged from around the side of the mansion, standing in the harsh glare.

The booming voice echoed through the mist. "What's going on here?"

"Mr. Forester," said Jake. "Thank goodness you're here."

Edward Forester looked down at his bare-chested son and the girl in the lavender dress. "My God. What have you done to him?"

"Brad's not right, Mr. Forester," Jake said. "He's lost his mind."

Brad grinned stupidly at his father. "Dad! Look, Alice has come back."

Mr. Forester shook his head. "The sheriff called me up at the farm to say there was some kind of trouble."

"It's over now," Jake said.

Mr. Forester took a step toward his son, but the panther raised itself up and growled at him. "Call her off, son. Come on, Brad-man. Call her off!"

"Alice, down!"

The cat sat back on its haunches again.

Mr. Forester looked into his son's eyes. "Brad, snap out of it."

But Brad only let out a childlike burst of laughter. "She's alive, Dad. I didn't hurt her."

"He tried to kill us, Mr. Forester," Jake offered. "Just ask Cassie. He tried to hurt us."

Cassie nodded. "He killed Alice Gilbert. He kidnapped my sister. You've got to get Brad some help, Mr. Forester."

Brad's father sighed deeply. "I can see that." Then he turned toward Jake. "I want you to tell me everything. But you'd better let me have that gun, Taylor. We wouldn't want anyone getting hurt."

Jake nodded. "Here. I'm sorry you had to find out about Brad like this."

He handed the weapon to Mr. Forester and explained what had happened. Then he moved toward Cassie. Andrea also ran to her sister. As they embraced, Mr. Forester took Brad's arm and led him away from the group.

"We better go back to the car," Jake said.

Cassie nodded. "Let's."

They turned toward the woods, all of them shaking with relief.

Edward Forester scowled at them. "Where do you think you're going?"

Jake looked over his shoulder. "We're going home and we're going to call the sheriff."

Forester thumbed back the hammer of the pistol, aiming it at Jake's chest. "You're not going anywhere, fella," he said coldly.

Jake stared down the barrel of the pistol. "What's the matter?"

A strange expression came over Mr. Forester's face. "You take one more step and I'll blow your brains out."

Jake's face went slack as he gaped in disbelief at Edward Forester. "What are you doing?"

"You're not leaving this estate," Forester replied. "You're not going to have my son arrested."

Cassie drew Andrea closer to her. "But Brad has hurt people, Mr. Forester. He set Jake on fire, he tried to throw me off a cliff. He kidnapped my little sister and locked her in the basement with that awful animal. He's mentally ill. You have to get him some help."

"Shut up! There's nothing wrong with my son."

Andrea cried out, pleading with the brutish man not to kill them. The panther turned its black eyes on the hulking figure with the pistol. A low growl escaped its throat. It sensed danger in the large man with the scowl on his face.

Edward Forester continued to hold the others at gunpoint. "You're not going to Hagen. I can't let you."

Brad stepped up next to his father. "Dad, Alice is alive. Look. I didn't hurt her, she's right there."

His father shook his head. "That's Cassie Arthur, you simpleton. She's dressed up like Alice. Are you so far gone you can't tell?"

"It's Alice, Dad. I didn't hurt her."

Forester sighed. "You fool. You stupid little jerk. You couldn't help yourself, could you?"

"No," Brad said, smiling dumbly. "It's Alice. I didn't hurt her, Dad."

"Shut up!" Forester snapped. "You've got to pull yourself together."

The man's harsh tone of voice caused the panther to rise again. Forester quickly stepped back. He made Brad tell the cat to lie down. The panther obeyed the command, but it still glared at the hulking man who seemed to threaten its master.

Brad grabbed the front of his father's shirt. "Dad, don't you see her? Alice is alive. I didn't hurt her."

"You idiot!"

The cat growled.

"Can't you see the truth?" Forester railed.

140

"These kids were on to you. They tricked you, Brad-man. And now they want to hurt you."

Brad pouted like a child. "No! That's Alice. She's my friend, Dad. I didn't hurt her!"

"Alice is dead!" Forester cried.

Jake stared accusingly at Brad's father. "You knew! You knew all along that Brad killed her?"

Forester scowled back at Jake. "The little tramp. She had it coming."

Brad screamed suddenly. He heard the words echoing in his head. A throbbing pain shot through his skull, forcing him to his knees. He held his head in his hands as the screeching cry brought the vision back to him. It all came into focus in his mind, the same way it had happened that other night.

"What's wrong?" Cassie cried.

Jake shook his head. "He's losing it again."

Brad saw the body of Alice Gilbert lying there in front of him. Blood trickled from her blue lips. The shadow appeared over her corpse. Brad turned but this time shadow figure didn't disappear. He saw his father standing over the body. Edward Forester then swung a bloody hand at his son, knocking him down next to Alice.

His father shook him. "Get up, Brad. Get up now!"

Brad came up slowly, turning toward his father. "You!" he cried. "You killed Alice. I remember now, Dad. It was you."

"Shut up, Brad! I mean it!"

Brad's eyes narrowed. "You hit Alice because she wouldn't give in to you. You were after her. She told me. You drove her away, Dad."

"It was an accident," Forester replied. "I didn't mean it, son. She lied to me. I just couldn't stand to hear her lies anymore, so I hit her. I didn't mean to kill her."

"You hit me, too," Brad said in a low voice. "I went out. When I woke up, you told me I had killed her. But I couldn't remember, so I believed you."

"No, son, that's not—"

"Bury her, you fool. That's what you said to me. You called her a little tramp. You said she had it coming. But you killed Alice because she wouldn't do what you wanted. Then you made me think I did it. You had me bury her in the trees. It was all *you,* Dad."

Edward Forester backed away from his son. "Brad-man, we've kept it a secret this long. No one has to find out just because of these kids."

"You killed Alice!" Brad cried. "Not me. *You* killed her!"

"Shut up! Shut up!"

The panther tensed, growling at the man who spoke gruffly to its master.

"You let me take the blame," Brad went on. "You let me think I killed Alice. But I didn't!"

Jake took the opportunity to lean forward. "He did it, Brad. Not you. He made you suffer even though you didn't kill anyone. Pay him back!"

"You're going to get it now, Taylor," Forester shouted.

Edward Forester lifted the pistol. But Brad lunged at his father, deflecting the angle of the pistol barrel as the shot went off. They struggled for a moment with the pistol between them.

"Now!" Jake cried.

He started to run, taking Cassie and Andrea with him. They bolted over the wet lawn, ducking around the side of the mansion. They headed for the iron gates at the entrance to the estate.

Edward Forester pushed his son away from him. "See what you've done, you fool? Stay here while I get them back."

The cat screeched from the shadows as the hulking man ran past.

Andrea couldn't run as fast as Jake and Cassie. She tripped on the wet grass, tumbling to the ground. Jake lifted her up and they started to run again, stumbling through the swirling fog.

Brad's red car was parked in the driveway ahead of them. They stopped when they came to it, but there were no keys in the ignition. Something made a panting noise behind them. Jake pushed Cassie and her sister toward the iron gates at the front of the estate.

Andrea took another fall in the grass. She was weak from her ordeal in the basement. Jake and Cassie had to carry her to the front gate.

"It's locked!" Cassie cried. "Brad's father has locked us in. We're trapped."

"Climb over!" Jake said. "Hurry, I'll give you a boost up."

"You aren't boosting anyone, you little creep!"

They turned to see Edward Forester pointing the gun at them again. He had caught them in the fog. Now he was going to kill them.

"Please," Cassie said. "Don't hurt us."

"You can't go free," Forester replied in a hateful voice. "I'm going to have to kill you, Taylor. I won't kill the girls. They'll be mine. They'll stay with me."

"No!" Cassie cried.

"Shut up, you little tramp. You led my son on and then you hurt him. But you're going to disappear, just like Alice Gilbert. Only you won't be dead."

"You'll never get away with it," Jake said. "We've already talked to the sheriff about Brad."

Forester laughed. "Hagen doesn't believe a word you told him. And I'll fix it so you look like the main suspect in the disappearance of all three girls." He turned to Cassie and Andrea. "Neither of you will ever be found."

"You're sick," Jake said.

Forester waved the barrel of the gun. "Move. I'm taking you back to the house."

"No, you're not."

The voice had come from behind them. Brad stood behind his father with the panther at his side. Brad's eyes were wide. Jake and Cassie had seen the expression on his face before, when he was trying to hurt them. Only this time, Brad's anger was focused on his father.

Forester backed up a little, smiling nervously. "Brad-man, hey—"

"You killed Alice!"

"No, I—"

"You called her a little tramp!"

"Son, please."

Brad pointed a finger at him. "You said she had it coming."

"Brad-man, it's me, your father."

"You've got it coming," Brad whispered.

"No!"

Brad looked sideways at the panther. "Alice, *kill!*"

The panther sprang through the mist, leaping toward the hulking man with the pistol. The gun exploded, flashing light in the fog. A piercing howl escaped from the panther's throat. The cat fell on top of Edward Forester, tearing at his soft neck with pointed white teeth.

Blood poured onto the moist ground. Edward Forester gulped for air, but he no longer had a throat. Brad stood over him, watching his father die.

Jake couldn't take his eyes away from the gory spectacle. "My God."

Cassie knelt down, shielding Andrea's eyes. She looked at Brad, wondering if he was going to hurt them. He still had a hideous expression on his rugged face. But then the panther rolled off the body, emitting a pitiful cry of pain.

"No!" Brad cried.

He saw the bullet hole in the animal's chest. His father's shot had hit its mark. Blood oozed from the wound as the animal lay on its side.

"Alice!" Brad said frantically. "He hurt you."

Jake and Cassie watched as Brad knelt next to

the wounded creature. The panther raised its head, making a pitiful sound. Brad began to stroke the creature's head, saying sweet words of comfort. The cat laid its head down one last time, breathing its final breath.

Brad sat on the ground, patting the neck of his dead friend. A low, moaning sound came from deep inside the tortured teenager. He stayed beside the panther's body until the sheriff's deputies came.

By the time they finally got Brad into the ambulance, he was sobbing and incoherent.

Chapter 14

Sheriff Hagen paced back and forth in front of Jake and Cassie. He kept them for a long time after the mess had been cleaned up. Sitting in the main parlor of the Forester mansion, they had told the story over and over. But the sheriff still wasn't sure that he could believe their unlikely tale.

Hagen snorted. "I don't know, Taylor. I arrive to find you and your girlfriend here. Ed Forester is dead. There's a panther that's been shot with a gun that belonged to your late father. Brad Forester has lost his mind and can't even talk to us about what happened. You had bad blood with the kid. It seems to me that you did this to him."

Jake shook his head, sore from exhaustion. "Mr. Forester killed Alice Gilbert, sir. Only he tried to make Brad think he had done it. When Brad remembered the truth, he sent the panther after his father. Mr. Forester fired the shot that killed the panther. I swear that's the truth."

"Where'd Forester get your father's gun?"

Jake lowered his eyes. "From me. I brought it here when we chased Brad, after he kidnapped Andrea."

Mrs. Arthur had already been to the estate to pick up her youngest daughter. She had taken Andrea to the hospital to be treated for shock. The sheriff hadn't insisted on Andrea staying behind for questioning.

Hagen sighed. "This just keeps getting weirder and weirder. You still insist that Brad survived that fall off the cliff?"

Jake nodded. "He said a wrecker pulled the car out of the bay and towed it over to Timberlake."

"We can check that," the sheriff said quickly.

"Go ahead," Jake replied.

Hagen raised a pink book in his hand. "One of my men found this in your car behind the back wall of the estate."

Cassie looked straight at the sheriff. "That's Alice Gilbert's diary. And I'm wearing her dress. Brad left them at my house."

"Why?" Hagen asked.

"Because he was crazy!" Cassie snapped. "Can't you understand that? His father drove him insane!"

She began to cry.

Jake put his hand on her shoulder. "Take it easy, Cassie. Imagine how it looks from the sheriff's point of view. I'm not sure I would believe any of it if I hadn't seen it with my own eyes."

"I want to go home," Cassie sobbed, tears running down her cheeks.

Sheriff Hagen shook his head. "No way. I'm going to have to take you down to the station and hold you there until we get this straightened out."

"I'm not sure that will be necessary, Sheriff Hagen."

The woman's voice filled the spacious parlor. They all turned to see Mrs. Forester standing in the archway. She was smoking a cigarette, and she tried to stand tall and proud in her own home.

Sheriff Hagen took a deep breath. "There's trouble, Mrs. Forester."

"I know," she replied coldly. "I just returned. I've been told that my husband is dead and my son has been taken away to the hospital."

The sheriff nodded. "Yes, ma'am. I'm sorry."

Mrs. Forester glanced toward Jake and Cassie. "I want to hear what these children have to say—"

Sheriff Hagen began to tell the story.

"—in their own words," Mrs. Forester insisted.

Even though they had been driven beyond exhaustion, Jake and Cassie managed to fill in the details one more time. Mrs. Forester listened patiently, drawing on her cigarette. When they were finished, she walked silently across the room and poured herself a drink.

"We're done here," the sheriff said to one of his deputies. "Take these kids down to the station house."

Mrs. Forester spun around to face the law officer. "No! If these kids are telling the truth, then the body of Alice Gilbert is buried somewhere on this estate."

Jake grew hopeful. "That's right, Mrs. Forester. In the trees at the back of the estate. Just get someone to look."

"Please," Cassie urged. "You have to believe us."

Mrs. Forester shot Hagen an icy look. "Do it, Sheriff. Quickly, before we all lose our nerve."

The sheriff squinted at the handsome, dark-haired woman. "What do you know about all this, Mrs. Forester?"

She averted her eyes to the side. "My husband kept many secrets from me, Sheriff. This is only one more, but it's the one that took my son away from me. I lost Brad thanks to my husband."

Cassie peered sympathetically at the distraught woman. "I'm sorry, Mrs. Forester. Brad wasn't all bad. He stopped your husband from killing us."

Mrs. Forester turned away from them. "You'll pardon me if I don't find any comfort in that fact. Sheriff, do your job quickly. I have a bad taste in my mouth."

Sheriff Hagen put his men to work. They began digging in the grove of trees near the stone wall. By late afternoon, they had found the remains of Alice Gilbert.

Chapter 15

The last day of school was beautiful and sunny. Jake Taylor stood in the hallway, cleaning out his locker. He had not quite recovered from the ordeal with Brad Forester, but he was feeling stronger than he had in the days since the bizarre incident. His spirits sagged drastically, however, when he saw Cassie walking straight toward him in the hallway.

Jake had not spoken to Cassie since the trouble at the mansion. He had seen her at Brad's hearing, when Brad was sentenced to go to the state mental hospital in lieu of criminal punishment. He had also seen her every day at school. But, somehow, their experiences with Brad had made them feel hesitant with each other.

Cassie walked up to Jake and smiled at him. "Hi there."

Jake blushed. "Hi. I was just cleaning out my locker."

Cassie sighed. "I went up to the hospital to see Brad."

Jake looked into his locker. "How is he?"

"He isn't doing well."

"That's too bad," Jake said.

Cassie looked into the locker. "Do you want some help?"

"Okay."

She helped him put his possessions into a cardboard box. Jake felt funny having her there next to him. He could smell the sweet scent of her hair. For a moment, it was almost as though nothing had happened.

Jake dropped a pair of sneakers into the box. "That's it."

Cassie looked into his eyes. "Do you think you could give me a ride home, Jake?"

"Sure."

"Let's go."

They walked silently down the hall. None of the other students at Cresswell knew what had really happened at the Forester estate. They had heard that Edward Forester died of a heart attack. And they knew that Brad had left for an early summer vacation. But everything else had been kept quiet, thanks to Sheriff Hagen and Mrs. Forester's bribe money.

When they got into the car, Cassie slid over next to Jake. "Did you hear Brad's mother is selling the estate?"

Jake put his hands on the steering wheel. "She really didn't know about Brad or her husband, I guess."

"Nothing they can prove anyway," Cassie replied.

Jake started the green Chevy. He put it into gear and drove away from his last day as a junior at Cresswell High. He hoped his senior year would not be nearly as harrowing.

Cassie sighed. "We're seniors now."

Jake nodded. "I don't suppose there's much to say. It's over."

Cassie frowned, looking out of the window. "Do you ever have dreams?"

"Every night," Jake replied.

"It's almost real again," Cassie said. "Andrea has them, too."

"How is she?"

"Better," Cassie replied.

"I'm glad. Tell her I said hello."

"Do you want to come over for dinner on Wednesday?" Cassie asked.

"Sure."

She patted his hand. "Jake, I want to take this slow. I'm not sure it's love, but we shared a great tragedy, and it's brought us closer. I think we should give it a chance. I've grown very fond of you."

"And I you," Jake replied.

He felt weak inside. She had almost confessed that she loved him. He thought he felt the same way. But it would take some time for them to find out if their feelings were real.

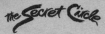